STARS IN THE HONEY

Kelsey Cantrell

For Mom and Dad

Chapter 1

Cool air drifted through a crack in the side door. Goosebumps developed under the sweat dripping down my bare leg, propping the door and letting the early March night creep into the bar. My pleather boot crunched up between the red metal door and frame and I wiggled it, making sure it was snug in its trap. I faced the outside air and inhaled, feeling the crisp bite at the back of my nose. Then, I turned to face the room again, letting the air reach around to my neck.

The Front Porch, a bar an hour and a half from my hometown of Danville, Indiana, felt nothing like a real front porch. Stuffed throughout the floor were tall circular metal tables with matching metal chairs and every concrete wall was plastered with white, gray, and black abstract murals. The ceiling seemed unfinished and silver metal lights hung at random, unmoving from the stagnant air inside. It was stuffy and smelled like dusty books and maple. The only thing that did resemble a front porch was the wooden floor, painted white like a suburban home exterior. At this point in the night, the floor had turned a spotty brown from clumsy alcohol spills.

To my left, toward the back of the room, stood a small wooden stage. A band dressed in all black was setting up their equipment: a mic stand at the front, amps near the back, a drum set in the middle. The girl setting up the mic stand lifted her head and pushed dark curls off of her forehead. She found me in the crowd and waved. I grinned, giving her a thumbs up.

Elena had been my best friend since she was born. Her mom and my mom were best friends growing up too, so when Elena was born two months after me, it was inevitable that we would be together always. And, being inseparable for eighteen years, of course I came to every single one of her shows.

Elena's boyfriend, Jack, stood behind her and started to tune his bass. He was at least a foot taller than her, if not more. It was hard to tell now because she had on heeled boots with her long flowing black dress. Jack's brown hair was slicked back on top of his head, which made his jawline even stronger than normal. His pouty lips turned up into a smile as he noticed me too and nodded in my direction.

Elena and Jack met at our high school. He was a year older than us, but they instantly clicked over their love of playing and singing music after officially meeting at an after school songwriting club. A couple months after their first date, they started the band, recruiting Jack's older brother, Wes, and Wes' friend Munro. A week into the band's start, they picked their name: Magnolia's Moon, after Elena's favorite flower and Munro's love for astronomy.

Elena stuck the microphone on top of the stand and turned around to see if the guys were ready. Wes and Jack stood attentive, armed with their guitars, and after a moment of looking around, the drummer walked on stage. Munro, tall and lanky with blonde hair, sat down behind his drum set. He had taken his glasses off before stepping on stage so it took me a moment to recognize him. Wes turned from his spot near the front of the stage and winked at Munro. He flashed a smirk back and situated himself on the tiny wooden stool.

Munro and Elena locked eyes and Munro nodded. Elena turned and stepped up to the mic. "Welcome, everyone. We're Magnolia's Moon and we're gonna start with a brand new one tonight, so I hope you like it," she said eloquently.

They started playing a song I had heard Elena sing a million times in the car, in the shower, and during free period. She wrote it months ago and just decided it was good enough to perform. The drums played softly and slowly in the background and the rings on Munro's fingers glittered as he moved. The guitar and bass started to bring up the excitement as Elena softly sang her first verses of a song I always loved called, "The Immortal Man."

"You're in a cloud of immortality,
The one you'll never even see.
The way you looked right through me
in that bar with shining moonlight scenes.
I never understood you didn't see a single part of me…"

Groups of people assembled at each table and some at the long wooden bar near the front door to my right. The bartenders, dressed in all black, shuffled around trying to get the impatient customers their Jack and Cokes or Long Islands.

I glanced down at my own outfit: a slinky silver slip dress and a black leather jacket I'd found at a Goodwill. About a year ago, I painted a Southern Magnolia on the back surrounded by tiny silver stars. Looking around again, I seemed to fit in enough. Everyone either dressed like they'd never seen a farm animal in their entire life, or they dressed so over-the-top cowboy that you wondered if they really lived in Indiana or visiting from a dude ranch in Texas.

After the first song ended, I found myself surrounded with onlookers and the wind outside had started getting too cold for my taste. As they started their next song, I clutched my studded crossbody bag to my stomach and shoved my way past leather-bound bikers and self-proclaimed hipsters wearing all different colors of suede and funky hats. A few guys watched as I passed by but I tried to avoid their gazes. One guy wearing a wide-brimmed cowboy hat winked and I scrunched my face up and kept moving. Everyone else watched the band set up or stared into their drinks longingly.

Finally, I reached the bar and pulled out my wallet. I handed the bartender my I.D. (a fake I'd gotten from Jack a couple years back). He looked at it, then at me, and back at the card. He handed it back. *Thank you, Isabel Williams, age twenty-one.*

"Whiskey sour, please," I said, straining over the noise.

The bartender nodded and started mixing. A stool emptied up so I grabbed it and sat down. He handed me my drink and I turned around to face the stage again. The crowd had surrounded me but I could see enough through them that I decided to stay and watch from the bar. About two hours later, I had ordered three more whiskey sours and started feeling a twinge in my stomach. My legs felt light.

Elena said her thanks to the crowd after their last song and waved before putting the mic stand away into a black case. The rest of the band started to put away their things too. I stayed by the bar as little groups of people started making their way outside, kicking my legs back and forth, rocking the stool. I took one last sip and turned to set

my last drink on the bar before I felt a light tap on my
shoulder.

"Hey, Seren. How'd you like the show?" Jack
asked as he and Munro walked up beside me.

"One of the best ones yet," I replied.

Jack carried his bass over his shoulder and Munro
carried a speaker between his hands. His drumsticks stuck
out the back pocket of his shorts. His clear framed glasses
sat on the bridge of his nose and they glistened under the
speckled light fixtures along the ceiling and the bar. All of
his features were soft except the area right around his thick
eyebrows and right under his chin. His dark blue eyes
settled deep into his cheeks. He wore a black cut-off tank,
black shorts, and high-top Vans.

"I'm glad you made it. I haven't seen you since
that party a while back," said Munro. His affable voice was
difficult to hear over the crowd.

"I'm glad I came too. It was a great set!" I strained back. One side of his mouth swung up for a second, and he went back to awkwardly swaying behind Jack.

"Do you need a ride home?" Jack asked, turning his keys over in his free hand.

"Yeah, uh, I think Elena was actually going to stay at my house tonight too," I said.

"Oh, right. Yep. She said that earlier." He paused and looked back to see how far Elena and Wes were getting with the set deconstruction. "Let me go throw this in my car real quick, and when I get back, we should all be ready to head out."

I nodded. "Sounds good to me."

I watched Jack and Munro struggle through the mass of people with the extra bulk in their arms and then turned my gaze back to the band. Elena stood near the front carrying a black case with one hand on her hip. She seemed like she was telling Wes what to do or to hurry up. He kneeled, picking up pieces and putting them into random cases.

Although brothers, Wes and Jack shared little resemblance. Wes had light green eyes and Jack's, a dark chocolate brown. Wes' hair had natural blonde streaks throughout and it feathered around his head in long waves, half covering his ears and forehead. Now, he had it partially styled upward to stay out of his face but the strands still seemed to have no order about them. It contrasted well with Jack's dark, slicked back style. They even dressed differently. Jack always looked sharp , usually a button-down shirt, a blazer, and funky loafers. Wes almost always sported distressed jeans and heavy combat boots. As he packed equipment away, I noticed the scruff lining his lips. His arms looked strong and veiny, covered in patches of colorful tattoos.

After what I assumed was another command from Elena, Wes sat back for a minute. He looked up at her, then caught me watching and rolled his eyes, laughing like an incorrigible toddler.

Once outside, Munro and Wes said goodbye to Elena, Jack, and I in front of our cars. The air was cold and damp and most of the sounds around us consisted of drunk girls stumbling into trucks and crickets in the woods that surrounded most of the parking lot.

"See you guys later!" Wes yelled, climbing into the driver's seat of his black Jeep. Munro waved and opened the passenger door. We all waved back as he stepped in. Once they started pulling away, we packed the last two bags into Jack's SUV and got in for the hour and a half drive home.

After leaving the parking lot, we drove down a couple streets of small businesses and coffee shops. Halfway home, I watched as dead cornfields turned into one long, tan blur. Patches of sparse grey trees interspersed them on the highway but it always came back to that hazy strip of beige death. Once we passed the haunted bridge

and the Danville Kroger, the cornfields were gone and

replaced with purposefully placed trees, broken sidewalks,

and small, crumbling colonial-style homes. We passed the

old high-school-turned-random-government-building that

also transformed into a not-so-scary haunted house during

October, the courthouse surrounded by tiny little shops no

one has ever heard of outside of Danville itself (besides the

Mayberry Cafe, of course: a whole restaurant dedicated to

"The Andy Griffith Show"), and finally, the library which

was decent enough that I actually worked there every

Thursday through Sunday.

Finally, we passed about ten more houses and

reached a hidden gravel driveway that led back into a patch

of trees to my house: a small one-story with a built-on

garage and one concrete step up to the front door. The

brick siding and dark green windows, door, and roof

seemed to disappear into the woods around it. A few of the

shingles were missing and one of the front windows in the

kitchen had a very noticeable crack right down the center. Remnants of a front garden traced the outer edge of the house and around to the side.

Jack pulled right up to the garage and parked, turning down the music he'd been playing. Elena and I said our thanks, me with an actual "thank you" and Elena with a few drawn-out kisses, and headed inside.

About an hour later, we were both changed into yoga clothes, hair up, makeup off. I sat on my mat in my room alone and stretched out my toes. My mind focused on the chipped, navy nail polish as the bones and muscles pulled and groaned under my skin. Wrinkles formed at the bridge of my nose - a cramp. I plunged my fingers into the tissue and rubbed until the pain went away.

Elena walked in with our steaming mint teas and I switched to the butterfly stretch, pushing my knees down with my elbows. Elena handed me my tea in a *Princess Bride* mug I had found at Goodwill a year before. I inhaled the steam. The tiny droplets dripped down the back of my nose.

She sat down next to me on her own mat, setting her tea up on the desk.

"Your dad was in the kitchen," she said.

I stared at my feet.

"He was getting coffee. He said hi and then went back out to the garden with his book. I feel like I haven't seen him in forever," said Elena, continuing without me. She lay back on her mat, lifting her legs into the air and letting them slowly float down. Her breath stayed slow and steady as she lifted them up again.

"Has he changed at all?" she asked, "I saw he's starting a beard."

I sat straight up and rolled my shoulders. "Not really," I said, laying back on my mat. Our ears settled only a couple inches away from each other.

"Do you ever join him out there?" she asked.

I shook my head and answered, "It's his space. You know how he is."

Elena sighed. She let her legs rest. "I just thought, you know, it could be a good bonding moment, sitting out there together and writing or reading. Just letting there be time with you together again."

I rolled my shoulders back, letting my arms lay a little away from my body, palms facing the ceiling. I stretched out my legs and let my feet fall to the side. "We're just not like that anymore," I said. I took a deep breath, in and out slowly. My body started melting down, grounding.

Elena moved her arm, letting her hand rest on top of mine. She gave it a little squeeze.

We lay there on our backs together, eyes closed, breathing in sync. Ingrid Michaelson's Human Again album played on shuffle softly off of my laptop up on the bed. I looked over at Elena. Her dark curly hair had been thrown up into a high bun on the top of her head, her makeup had faded off her tan skin from the day and the sweat, and her full lips pressed together as she thought about breathing and whatever else was going on in her beautiful mind.

I closed my eyes again and started to focus. Three full seconds in, three full seconds out. I pictured my dad sitting in the garden. It was a small square space, about six feet by six feet with a cobblestone floor he put in when I was three. Surrounding the garden were tall, wooden grid arbors laced with vines and yellow and white honeysuckle and white hydrangea. A rounded archway led out from the garden to a stone pathway that wrapped around and led up to the back porch and our sliding glass doors in the living room. In the middle of the garden sat a small wooden table, a little lopsided from being homemade and worn down. And behind it, against one of its flowered walls, sat a dark green armchair, stained and ripped but still as comfy as any other armchair. It only got wet during really hard storms because Dad had built a wooden awning over that half of the garden a few years after he put down the cobblestone. My dad would sit in the chair with his reading glasses on, balancing on the edge of his nose. A dusty novel or a composition notebook would lay in his lap or on the little table and eventually he would doze off. He could even be asleep right now but I would never know. Every once in a while, I would hear him shuffle in around two or three in the morning and climb into his creaky bed in the room next door. Once I woke up again though, he would be back out in the garden.

After a few songs, Elena shifted, bringing her legs up to her chest into a fetal position. Her knees brushed my hip. She took in a deep breath and sighed as she let the air escape from her body again. "Wes looked pretty hot tonight, didn't he?" she asked.

I glared. "Look, I know I had this, like, huge crush on him freshman year or whatever, but you don't have to bring it up every time I see you guys play," I said.

"Okay, okay," she said, smiling to herself.

We stared up at the ceiling together, breathing in and out.

"Are you ready for bed?" she whispered. "We have school in the morning, after all."

I nodded and she stood, helping me up along with her. "We need to change. These yoga clothes are ripe," she said. She pulled off her tank top and tossed it into my laundry basket across the room. We changed into shorts and giant tattered t-shirts, and I jumped under the pastel yellow comforter on my bed. Elena turned off the lamp and climbed in after me. Heat radiated off of her body and I felt it blush my cheeks. Her dark curls cascaded over the pillow.

"I'm gonna miss you, Lena," I whispered.

"It's not for forever," she answered. She shifted and our legs touched.

"It'll feel like it."

Her socked foot rubbed against my shin. "Don't think about it too much. We still have to worry about graduating first. Which means…sleep," she said, poking me in the arm, eyes still closed. "Goodnight for now, Seren. I'll see you when I wake up." She situated her body, stretched out straight, one arm under the pillow.

"Goodnight for now. See you in the morning," I said back. I turned to face the wall, curling my legs up to my chest. I glanced up at the poster above my side of the bed. Magnolia's Moon stood triumphantly in front of a black background in all black clothing, holding their instruments. I had made the poster for their first gig ever and in just three months, they'd be going on a summer tour all across the Midwest.

I tried to stop thinking about it. My fingers traced the cracks in the baby blue paint under the poster until I was too tired to hold them up anymore. And then, hearing Elena's heavy breathing behind me, I fell asleep too.

The next morning Elena slept in, and I got up to make coffee. Sometimes my dad would already have a pot lying out for me, just one cup gone from it. Other days,

he'd make tea or just grab a quick snack and a water before

going to the garden.

I walked out of my bedroom, being careful not to

trip over clothes or open the door far enough to where it

creaked. Then I made it down the hallway, past my dad's

room and the bathroom and into the living room. I passed

the front doorway on my left. Then I glanced to my right

through the living room and out the glass doors. They were

open and a brisk breeze crept into the room.

I kept walking toward the kitchen, feeling the

carpet warm up my feet. I had always thought our kitchen

was cool. It had two open doorways, one on either side of

one wall that both led out into the living room. Then a

weird glassless window that stretched from each open

doorway just high enough to where you could reach up and

glance through it. The window acted like a shelf and my

mom had always kept her mug collection there.

I made my way to one of the doorways and realized the kitchen lights were on. I peeked my head in. My dad stood facing the window to the side of the house, back to me. He wore his robe and slippers and graying hair poked out in every direction.

"Good morning, Dad," I whispered, leaning against the doorway.

He turned and let loose a small smile. Then he gestured to the mug in his hand and said, "Good morning. I made some tea."

"I was gonna make coffee. Elena's here," I replied.

"Late night then, I assume?" he questioned.

I nodded silently and shifted against the doorway.

"Ah, I'll get out of your hair then," he said, moving away from the counter. He grabbed a spoon from a drawer and walked out the other doorway to the garden, shutting the sliding doors behind him. I moved to the coffee maker on the counter and started it. Then I hopped up onto the counter and waited.

Before my mom left us, my dad worked at home half the time and in New York City the other half for a publishing company. For a couple weeks, he'd stay home and read and edit other peoples' work while sometimes working on his own writing too. Then for a couple weeks, he'd take a plane to New York and work in his office there and have meetings all the time.

When he was home, he made sure to spend as much time with my mom and me as possible. We would go see movies at the theater or go to vintage car shows (which I never really liked other than seeing all of the cool new paint jobs, but I liked seeing him get excited). Every Saturday morning he was home, we'd go to the same pancake house and order chocolate milkshakes and chocolate chip waffles with two over-easy eggs each on the side. We'd stuff our faces and then proceed to whatever activity he had planned for the day.

A lot of things changed after my mom left. The biggest thing was my dad. He stayed home from work for a few months. He didn't speak unless it was replying to voicemails from work saying if he didn't respond at all, he'd be fired. If he wasn't lying in bed staring at the empty spot next to him, he was in the garden writing the same things over and over again and then throwing away the papers as soon as he came inside. I fished some of them out once. Every inch of the pages were covered in doodles of the moon and stars and constellations and scribbled words about the universe.

I don't think my dad said anything to me for three or four months other than telling me Elena's mom was there to pick me up for school whenever I was running late. I became the most independent an eleven-year-old could be. Sometimes I'd ride my bike the fifteen minutes to school because I didn't want to bother asking Elena's mom to take me for what felt like the millionth time. Most days after school, I went home with Elena or straight to the library where I'd stay until a few hours after dark. Most lunches were deli meat sandwiches and whatever fruit we had lying around. Most dinners were microwavable.

I became scared of moving pretty soon after. I thought maybe my dad wouldn't be able to handle seeing everything my mom left behind every day. But instead, I think we both ended up clinging to those things to keep us sane. He hasn't moved her clothes or her shoes lying in a row against the wall of their bedroom. He's kept every piece of art she's done and hung on the wall. He hasn't even changed the pink mosaic tile on the bathroom floor even though he hated it so much when she remodeled the entire bathroom my second grade year. Instead of scaring us off, her lingering presence kept us grounded, at least for a while.

Slowly, my dad started seeming a little more like himself. One night when I was thirteen, he came into my room at around 2 in the morning. I laid on the floor in my pajamas writing and doodling like he always did. He knocked lightly on my door and it creaked open.

"Seren?" he whispered.

I looked up, straining my neck to see his face, six feet above me. I said nothing. I honestly didn't even know if he had actually said something to me or if I imagined it.

"Why are you awake? You have school in the morning," he continued. His voice was softer than it used to be. I could tell he wasn't mad.

"I wasn't tired. I can try now though," I stated.

He watched quietly as I folded my notebook closed and stood up, making my way over to my desk. I set the notebook down and turned to him. We watched each other for a moment, like we hadn't ever seen one another before. He had the darkest circles under his eyes. His mouth opened the slightest bit like he wanted to tell me something — maybe something about my hair being shorter, from the haircut Elena and I attempted with kitchen scissors a couple weeks earlier, or maybe something about the dark eyeliner I smeared across my top eyelid and the remnants of the dark lipstick I wore to school.

He didn't say either of those things. Instead, he just whispered, "Goodnight, Seren. Sleep well."

I watched him leave without saying anything back. Then I climbed into my bed and let tears fall down my face because I realized the man that used to be my father was gone and he wasn't going to come back, no matter how many nights I waited.

Chapter 2

"It hasn't come yet," I complained during free period. Elena and I sat in the soccer field next to one of the goals, both with notebooks sprawled open around us. Hers held scribbly song lyrics and mine contained lists and mood board collages and storyboards. A couple of guys from our year kicked a ball into the other goal, grunting and whooping more than talking. The sun was shining and the grass was thick and green and just a week into March, it was finally feeling like spring in Indiana.

"Maybe they send out their letters later than other schools," Elena said, shrugging. Even in a dress, she had her legs curled up to her chest. She held a copy of *Norwegian Wood* in her hands, resting on her knees. Her hair was pulled up into a high curly bun again. Two dark curls framed her tan cheeks and her green eyes looked wild as she scanned each page. "What about the other schools you applied to?" she questioned.

"I got both of their letters. One I didn't get in to. And the other I just really don't want to go to. It was the 'fallback' school that all of our teachers insisted I had to have... but it doesn't even have a film program so there's nothing there for me," I answered.

"Hm. Like I said, maybe their dates are different or the mail people screwed up," she replied. I groaned, running my hands down my face.

"Would it be weird to write a song about a fictional character? Cause I think I'm in love," Elena said, changing the subject so I wouldn't stress about it anymore. She tapped on the book cover with her fingers.

"Do it," I encouraged.

She lied back into the grass and turned over to face her notebook. "Okay. Here we go." She bookmarked the page with a flyer from our favorite coffee shop downtown.

Then she grabbed a purple pen from her bag and started writing.

"I just want it to come already. Every time I come home to the mail, it's just a stack of letters from my dad's company. I just need my stupid acceptance letter so I don't have to be in this town anymore," I said as one of the soccer boys kicked the ball and it rebounded off a goal bar. It bounced just a couple feet away. Harvey, a boy in our grade with long blonde hair and a pink face trotted over to grab the ball back.

"Hey, Seren. Hey, Elena," he said. "I saw your show the other night."

"Oh, that's great. What'd you think?" she replied, barely taking her eyes off her notebook to look up at him.

"You guys were so cool." He picked the ball up and tossed it between his hands.

"Thanks," she said quietly, continuing to write.

He stood around a moment longer.

"Not to be rude, but we're kinda trying to write. Could you go back to kicking?" She looked up at him and gave him a big soft grin and he smiled back.

"Right. See you later," he replied, understanding because it was Elena and no one could ever find Elena anything less than amazing.

Elena looked back over at me and smiled, shaking her head.

"Don't worry. It'll come. Just write some. That always calms you down," she said, continuing our interrupted conversation. She glanced up from her notebook and tapped my arm with her pen.

I looked down at a blank page. I wondered if that would be my future. Blank. It's exactly how I pictured my mom thinking about her own future. With nothing left in it at all. "I just can't write right now. Not yet," I said. I laid down next to Elena on my back, feeling the grass scratch against my neck and my bare thighs in my shorts. The sun seared my cheeks.

I pulled my shoulders under me and my palms fell toward the sky. My legs stretched out long and strong, and then the weight of them drifted to the ground. I let my eyes flutter shut. I started to think about my mom and how I remembered her from before she left.

Her name was Elodie, named after her mom, her mom's mom, and her mom's grandma who immigrated from France. My mom liked her name, but wanted a change so she gave the name to me too, just as my middle name instead. She picked Seren for its meaning: star. She had always loved the night for the moon and the stars and how alive she felt in the darkness.

Not only did I inherit her name and her love for the night, but I also got her platinum hair, her pink skin, her 5'9" height and thin frame, and her small upturned nose. I gained her love for adventure too, even though she never got the chance to leave. She grew up in the same little town of Danville, Indiana. She went to the same elementary school, the same middle school where she met Elena's mom, Vivian, and the same high school where she graduated as valedictorian with distinctions in English and art. For college, she traveled a state away and studied at the School of Art Institute of Chicago where she met my dad. After graduation, they moved back and had me a year later.

Most of the time when I was younger, it was just me and my mom since my dad was in New York a lot. Every day, starting at dinner, she would turn on a new movie. Some nights they were appropriate for kids and some nights they weren't. Neither of us minded either way. A lot of the inappropriate things (or things deemed inappropriate by stricter parents) just made me curious and my mom would always explain anything I didn't understand to the best of her ability. Some movies we watched over again and sometimes even three times like *The Big Sleep*, *Stand By Me*, and *Psycho*. Others we both really didn't enjoy like *Risky Business* and *Dr. Strangelove*.

One night, she put on *Dead Poets Society*. At seven years old, I didn't understand a lot of it but I thought the teacher was wacky and I laughed at his antics. Near the

end, one of the students somehow died. I didn't really

understand what happened but my mom sat on the couch

and cried. I walked over and maneuvered myself into the

space between one of her arms and her warm chest. She sat

there crying and stroking the hair tucked behind my ear,

and I sat there trying to figure out why. I missed most of

the end watching my mother's tears fall slowly onto her

shirt. I never asked. After that night, we watched that film

at least once a month and every time, she cried. I

eventually got the ending. I never cried at it before, and

now I can't watch it at all.

Before school every day, she would read me

fifteen pages of a book. I would watch her intently while

eating eggs and ketchup or pancakes smothered in peanut

butter. She'd pace around the room, acting out some of the

movements of the characters. I'd laugh at the jokes and

jump when my mom ran around the island to tickle my

neck, acting like a monster. On the way to school, we'd

listen to Fleetwood Mac or Duffy or the *Coyote Ugly*
soundtrack and belt every word with the windows down
until it turned too cold to stand.

On the way home, she'd say, "Tell me every detail
of your day, my love." And I would, starting with what
Elena and I did at recess. It usually took me the whole
fifteen minute ride to the house, but if not, it was back to
LeAnn Rimes singing "Can't Fight the Moonlight".

When I turned eleven, I could finally sit with her in
the front seat. It was my second day of sixth grade and I
was already dreading seeing everyone but Elena in my
classes. On the way to school, my mom suddenly stopped
singing right in the middle of her favorite song, Duffy's
"Syrup and Honey" and pulled into a playground parking
lot. She looked over at me. "I can't keep it inside anymore,
Seren," she said. With one hand on my bare knee she
continued, "You're getting a brother." She hadn't even told
my dad yet. The rest of the day I couldn't focus on

anything else. I had never necessarily wanted a sibling, but when she said the word "brother" my heart skipped.

After school, she told my dad and then I asked her all of the questions I could possibly think of which was really just: "How long do I have to wait?" She said she was almost five months along and that I'd have to wait just a few more.

One month later, he had a name: Orion. "Another addition to my own little galaxy," she said, smiling as big as I'd ever seen.

Then the next month came. Month seven. My dad was away and Elena's mom drove me home because my mom had a doctor appointment schedule at the same time I got off school. I noticed my mom's car in the driveway and thought that she must have been running late. After saying bye to Elena and Vivian and climbing out of their car, I ran into the house. When I walked in, the door shut behind me, and I couldn't hear her shuffling around anywhere. Then I called for her, but I didn't get an answer so I went looking.

Stars in the Honey

I found her sitting on the floor in the bathroom.
The whole room smelled of metal. Baby Orion was a smear
of blood on the white tile and she sat there, silent,
mindlessly spreading the red mess around with her fingers.
I tried to get her attention but she just stared at the patterns
in the floor, red-orange constellations spread out across the
pink tile. She didn't answer until I said her name for the
ninth time. Even then, she didn't move. She looked up at
me, eyes blank. I helped her up and into the shower. She
wouldn't stand, so I made sure she could sit up
comfortably against the wall. I turned on the water. The
room smelled even worse after the water started to steam. I
knew she wouldn't move on her own, so I left and called
Vivian.

She was there just ten minutes later and made
Elena and I stay in my room while she took care of my
mom the rest of the night. Neither of us talked. We laid in
my bed, side by side, holding hands and staring at the
ceiling until we both eventually fell asleep.

For about a week, she stayed in bed after getting the doctor's orders. My dad took the first flight home to take care of her, and until he got there, Vivian and Elena stayed over. My mom didn't have a weekday job, just weekend shifts at the library, so we didn't have to worry about losing much money. She stayed in bed, ate a lot of soup, and bread and butter, and tea. My dad lied by her side for most of it and he read passages out of her favorite books for her until she dozed off.

After the doctor's ordered week, she seemed to get better. She drove me to and from school every day again for about a month. We still watched movies and read books and sang together. But there was always this distant stare on her face when she thought I wasn't paying attention.

That month went by fast and then she started sleeping in and asking Vivian to pick me up or Dad to take me to school again. Sleeping in all morning turned into her sleeping all day. She didn't eat unless my dad or I brought a plate of something to her and even then, she'd barely touch it. We had doctors come and prescribe her medications and try to talk to her. Nothing seemed to work.

After a few months, I was staying at Elena's house almost full time because it was easier than picking me up and dropping me off every day. Her parents didn't care. Vivian and Gio always loved having me over, but I could tell they worried that I would never be able to go back to a normal home again.

My dad stayed home that entire time, working through his laptop and long phone calls. But soon it wasn't enough and he had to go back to New York. He left on a Friday afternoon, just for the weekend. On Monday, he came home and found his bed empty. He searched the house and found a note stuck to our copy of *Dead Poets Society*. It said, "I love you both but I'm joining our lost little star in the sky."

She left the sliding doors to the backyard open so he would know to look outside. He found her ten feet back in the woods, hanging from a branch. My dad had never said anything about it. I learned everything from a cop that asked me vague questions about my mom's depression that night.

Since then, I hadn't heard my dad say one more thing about my mom. He never said what happened after he found her. He never played her favorite music, never made peanut butter pancakes, never sat in her spot on the couch. He never said her name.

I needed to stop thinking about it. My eyes hurt. I opened them and saw the branches hanging over one side of the field. They were long skinny shadows in front of the bright sun.

"Soccer boys are leaving. Time for fifth period," Elena said. She laid her head on my stomach. I nodded without moving my gaze. Elena got up and I heard her pack up her things. After the rustling stopped, she stood in front of the sun, holding everything in her arms. The orange light haloed her face and the branches looked like a crown around her curls.

"Up, up, up," she insisted.

"Okay, okay. I'm getting up," I groaned.

The first class after free period was the absolute worst to endure.

Gym.

We were required to take two athletic courses during our high school careers and I put mine off until the very last minute. Not only did I have to attempt physical activity, I had to interact with humans other than Elena. She had an elective studying animal biology and health. That didn't sound much better, but at least she got to sit at a desk the whole time and wear her own clothes.

In the girls' locker room, I slowly and quietly changed into the ugly gym uniforms the school provided: red basketball shorts with DHS written on one leg and a gray t-shirt with our mascot, a "warrior," in red on the front. After everyone else had already walked out to the gym, I figured I should follow. I trudged out and sat in my designated spot on the basketball court sideline to wait for our teacher, Mr. Finnegan, to start talking.

"Afternoon, class," he began as he paced back and forth down the court. "We're gonna start with laps."

The entire class groaned and started standing up to take their place in the path around the court. As we started jogging, Mr. Finnegan yelled, "You know the drill. Every time I lap you while I'm jogging, I drop your letter grade for today's participation." He paused as we all turned to look back at him. "That means run!" he yelled and started jogging behind us.

I moved my legs as fast as I could for a while, making sure Mr. Finnegan was at least a good half-a-lap behind. He had already passed the two known-slackers in the class, Brian and Matt. They trudged behind Mr. Finnegan making faces and rolling their eyes. I kept right up behind the second fastest group. There was the first group: the try-hard girls that actually ran track and field

and then the second group, the guys and girls that couldn't

stand to get anything lower than an "A-" in anything. I'd

like to think I didn't like getting anything lower than a "C,"

but also, I despised the third group that always trailed

behind me. If I decided to try hard enough, I could skip the

second group and not have to worry about the third. But by

this time in the semester, I was already used to third

group's torment enough to not really care anymore.

The third group consisted of four guys and one

girl, who everyone said had gone through and slept with all

of the guys the first month of school when they all became

friends. Her name was Lexi and she made sure her bleach

blonde hair was stuck in a fluffy bun right on top of her

head at all times. Every day in gym, I would get some

comment or some unwarranted touch from one of the guys

and Lexi would watch with a smirk on her over-tanned

face.

Today, I just waited. And finally, one of the guys, Robert, spoke up. He wore his dark brown hair too long in the front that it almost covered his eyes and it always looked greasy, enough to where you could picture a drop of the oil sliding down his forehead into one of his eyes.

"Hey, Seren. We're having a bonfire at Mike's tomorrow," he said, making his way up to my pace and gesturing to one of the other guys in the third group.

"I'm good," I stated.

"Oh, come on. We're gonna play strip pool. Mike's got a table in his barn," he said. Lexi smirked and made eye contact with Mike.

"No, thanks," I said. I kept my eyes on the ground, following the thick white lines around the court.

"Whatever," he said, finally backing off to the group again. Then he whispered to Mike, "Said she can't. Gotta stay home and take care of daddy so he doesn't kill himself too."

My breath escaped all in one shove. I couldn't breathe.

I stopped running and rested my hands down on my knees. After just a second, a hand smacked against my ass and I jumped forward slightly. I knew it was coming. It wasn't a surprising moment when one of the guys in the third group did something like that.

I rested my hands back down on my knees.

"Seren. B," said Mr. Finnegan as he passed, just a few feet behind the third group.

I need to get out of here.

When the last bell rang, I packed up my backpack and trudged through the back hallway, trying to avoid as many people as possible. I reached the student parking lot and spotted my little rusty red Volkswagen near the back. Elena's black Jeep sat next to mine, and I looked around for her with no relief. Once I reached my car, I threw my backpack in and stood by the trunk, juggling my keys until Elena walked out one of the school doors.

She saw me and grinned. As she walked, she swung her backpack off one shoulder and pulled out her book from earlier. A little out of breath from walking, she said, "I finished it in biology. It's heartbreaking and wonderful. Do you want it next?"

I nodded. She got to her car, threw her backpack in the backseat, and tossed the book over the car. I caught it, smoothing down the green and white paper cover. Then I walked to the driver's side of her Jeep and leaned against it by the back wheel.

"How was gym today?" she asked.

I looked up from the book and laughed out loud. "It sucked a lot," I said.

Elena smiled but shook her head, knowing exactly what had happened without me even telling her. "Well, I gotta go home fast. Jack wants to make an early movie tonight," she said, shimmying a bit next to her open door.

"But I definitely want to know all of the details," she added.

I nodded and turned to walk back to my car. "Okay. Text me, love you," I said.

"Text me, love you!" she answered. She got into her car after our usual send-off and slammed the door shut. The engine roared and I could hear faint music coming from inside. She backed up, waved through the window, and sped off.

I looked down at the book again and ran my finger over the raised title. I knew if Elena liked a book, I would too. I tossed it into the passenger seat and got in my car.

At home, I pulled up the gravel driveway shrouded with trees and stopped in front of the garage. The house looked small and empty, although I knew my dad had been home all day and was probably still home, just out in the garden now. I turned the engine off and stepped out. The gravel crunched under my boots. I walked to the front door, my backpack hanging loosely off one shoulder. When I reached the front door, it was cracked so I pushed my way in. It was dark per usual.

Walking in, I kicked off my Dr. Martens boots by the front door and walked into the living room. I set my backpack on the tan corduroy couch, pulling off my jean jacket too. I didn't hear my dad anywhere. I walked around the back of the couch and around the wall to the kitchen. Next to the coffeemaker sat a dark red envelope.

"Dad!?" I yelled through the halls.

I picked up the envelope and touched my finger to the gold lettering. It read: "NYFA Admissions" and gave their office address underneath.

"Dad!? Are you home?" I strained my voice. Finally a light shuffling came from outside. The glass doors slid open in the living room and my dad trudged around the wall into the kitchen.

He pushed his glasses up into his curly graying hair. "Yes?" he said, giving off the slightest smirk. He knew exactly what I was holding.

"It came," I said, staring at the envelope in my hands. "I should open it."

My dad walked to the counter in his gray button-down, corduroy pants, and slippers, and leaned against it, letting his elbow rest on the granite. I flipped the envelope over in my hands, feeling the smooth, thick paper between my fingers. As I tore open the flap, I felt the glue strain between the sides. Inside was a plain sheet of white paper, folded into thirds. I set the envelope on the counter and pulled open the letter.

"Dear Seren E. Moore,

We regret that we are not able to offer you admission to the New York Film Academy Bachelor of Fine Arts in Filmmaking program..."

After that, I stopped reading. The rest of the page looked blank, completely white. A fuzzy darkness surrounded the paper.

"Well?" My dad's voice pierced the room.

I stared for a minute more. Then I folded the paper back into thirds. And I looked up.

"I got in." The words choked me, sliding out of my mouth like a snake escaping its tank.

My dad's mouth turned up into a grin. His teeth stayed hidden. It was one of the biggest smiles I'd seen from him since she left. He walked over to me, stopped at my side, and rested a hand on my shoulder. I looked into his eyes, the same dark hazel as my own. "I'm proud of you," he said. Then he walked back out the glass doors to the garden.

I couldn't feel my feet or my ankles or my knees and I fell to the ground, folding in on myself. Using the cabinets to lean against, I wrapped my arms around my legs and let everything go. Every time I had wanted to cry in the last few months came to me all at once and streams of saltwater ran down my cheeks and dripped into my lap.

"Fuck," I whispered into my knees.

The paper laid in my hand like a cheating lover in my bed and I crumpled it with that one hand and chucked it across the room.

Chapter 3

The next day was a Saturday and instead of feeling excitement for the weekend, the world felt small. I felt small. My room had suddenly compacted into a minuscule box, jailing me inside, all alone with my creeping thoughts. After waking up on my own at six A.M. and lying in bed for three more hours trying to sleep, my body needed to move. I had to get out of my room. I had to get out of that house.

It was an unusually cold day for March and at nine in the morning, the air was crisp and frost still settled across the back deck. I walked carefully across the wood and down the steps that led me to the edge of the garden. I peeked my head in. My dad's armchair was empty.

But the garden wasn't nearly far enough. I could still hear the walls of the house begging me to stay inside, begging to let them suffocate me. So I walked further into the woods, passing the rotting trees. I didn't know which one she swung from eight years ago but I didn't think it mattered either. They were all just pieces of wood that helped her get away. I guess the forest was helping me do the same now.

Eventually, I made it out to a pond that my dad and I found when I was little. I had forgotten about it, but now that I looked at it again, it felt free and open just like before. Just about ten feet wide and a foot deep to the very middle, the pond was a perfect pool. Dark leaves floated across the top. A chilling breeze drifted through the trees surrounding the edges of the water. Branches shivered above me.

I untied and slipped off my shoes, and even though I knew it would be too cold, I stepped into the water. Its murky, shimmering surface parted the way for my polished toes. Instantly, chills rose up to my shoulders. But it felt good.

As I shook, wiggling my toes in the frothy water, I remembered how I was when I was younger. I could go outside in nothing but my underwear and roll around in the snow. I never really felt the cold but the freedom the rebellion gave me sent shivers through my body.

I remembered my mother caught me once. She picked me up and ran inside, calling out for my dad, and wrapped me up in a dark red, fleece blanket and told me I was being dangerous. But it didn't feel dangerous. It felt real and simple and exciting. My mind strained to ask but I was shivering too hard to talk as I warmed up. I remembered her saying, "My bright star, you're meant for the sky, not the snow." Recently, I felt like I belonged in bed, covered in a blanket, hidden away from anything too close or too real or too fast.

I found myself now in nothing but my black t-shirt and blue, boy-short underwear and I sat down, in that freezing water, half-naked. And then I laid my entire body down. For a minute or two I shivered, and then I really thought about it. I thought about the goosebumps on my

thighs, little polka-dots raised up on my pale skin. I thought

about my lips turning purple. And I thought about the

twitching in my back between my shoulders, creating

ripples in the water around me. I relaxed. I forgot

everything. I forgot about New York and Elena and my

mother and father and I just looked straight up into the

almost covered gray sky, and then I was fine. Just fine. It

was simple again.

I thought about the clouds, the canopy of ashy

trees, the water sloshing against my moving legs, the slow

sprinkle of rain beginning to fall over my eyelids. My

feelings were gone and my chest opened up to a new world

of bliss, a normalness I often didn't feel.

I don't know how long I was lying there. I became

too numb to move my fingers so I decided it was best to

get out. After layering my clothes back on, I trudged back

through the woods to my room. I stripped the clothes back

off and threw them on the floor, changing into some fluffy

sweats and a long sleeved t-shirt I got for free at a school football game. My feet still felt frozen. I scavenged through the pile of mess on my floor and came up with one purple and one blue fuzzy sock. Finally, I was starting to feel mobile again.

"Seren…" My head whipped around to my door frame. My dad stood there, wrapped in a blanket and holding two cups of something steamy. "I made tea," he said.

I nodded for him to enter and replied, "Thanks, Dad."

He nodded back, stepping just inside the door, and took a sip. His head shook and he said, "Too hot still." I let a small grin slip through. He wore his red robe, a black Fleetwood Mac tee, and black sweatpants with slippers. His eyes sunk behind his glasses.

"Do you have any plans today?" he asked, lingering by the open door.

I shook my head.

He pressed his lips together before attempting another sip. This time, he just nods toward me. I take a sip. It was a comfortable heat. Chamomile, lemon, and honey.

He gives me one more look over, turns around, and then turns around again. "Did you take a shower?" he asked, pointing to his head, indicating that my hair was wet from my philosophical swim in the pond.

I nodded.

"Hm, I didn't hear the water." He shrugged. "I'll be out in the garden if you need me." He turned, shutting the door just enough to where a sliver of darkness still lingered at the edges.

"Thanks, Dad," I whispered, watching his thin frame shut my door behind him.

Sunday, I stayed in bed. In sweats and a baggy t-shirt, with my comforter pulled to my chin, I stared at the film and band posters taped to every inch of my walls. Instead of being motivation like I intended, every character and artist just stared back, judging me. I avoided Elena's band's poster altogether.

Halfway through the day, I rolled onto my back. I couldn't look at their eyes anymore so I opted for the ceiling. It was plain, white, and dotted with little yellow glow-in-the-dark stars that stopped glowing years ago. I traced constellations with my eyes until I fell asleep.

When I woke up, the only light left came from a small, full moon lamp on my desk. I looked at the pale yellow digital clock next to the lamp: 2:42 AM. I tried closing my eyes again but it had been over twenty-four hours and my stomach begged me to feed it. I threw off my covers and stepped onto the wooden floor.

I opened my door and the whole house was dark. Shuffling my way down the hallway and into the living room, I noticed a flashing white-yellow light reflecting onto the couch. My dad had wilted into a pillow against one arm, glasses still perched on his nose. A novel and a notebook lay in front of him on the coffee table. I walked over and reached for the glasses. Slowly, I pulled them off his face and folded them up, laying them on the coffee table. He didn't budge. I grabbed a blanket from the armchair by the window and laid it gently along his curled body.

Then I turned to the TV. Robin Williams as Mr. Keating stood on top of his desk, instructing his students to do the same. My next breath stuck in my chest and I turned around, scavenging for the remote. I checked the couch around my dad, his hand, carefully under the pillow.

"Shit," I whispered.

I checked the coffee table but all I found was a couple books and an almost-empty coffee cup.

Where is it?!

I started to panic. I didn't want to hear any more of Mr. Keating's words. When he spoke, all I heard were my mom's cries, the whimpers into the quilt my grandma made her that's now folded up on the window bench by the sliding doors, probably never to be moved again.

Finally, I found it. The remote had fallen on the floor in front of my dad. I picked it up and hit the power button with a shaky finger. The only light left came from the moon shining through the windows from the backyard. A white reflection fell onto Dad's cheek. His soft snoring permeated the silence. I watched him, chest moving up and down. I didn't feel like eating anymore and walked back to my room.

The first day back at school I wanted to avoid Elena. It was easy until free period. I just slipped to my locker before she could reach me and then slip away to class again. But for free period I didn't know where to go so we met up at the soccer field like normal.

It was a cloudy day, gray mist rolling across the white sky above us. A slight breeze rustled the tree leaves but the air felt warm and smelled musty.

She held her hand out in front of me, pointer finger up. "Sit," she demanded.

I sat. The damp grass stuck to my bare legs.

"I know you're still freaking out about your NYFA letter but right now we are going to write and watch the boys fuck up their stupid soccer kick moves like everything is fine and normal." She dropped her notebooks and pens into the grass. I sat down. She sat down in front of me and opened her notebook.

"Anything exciting happen this weekend?" she asked.

As I sat down to join her, I thought about the letter and the pond and the movie and how much I slept and didn't eat but instead of saying anything, I just opened one of my notebooks. I grabbed a green pen from my bag and started to doodle across a page. Then I shrugged and gave some kind of barely audible grunt.

"Okay, well that sounds exciting," she said sarcastically.

I looked up at her. She still scribbled in her notebook but a little more forcefully now.

"I called off work all weekend. Wasn't feeling great," I tried. My saliva felt thick like syrup dripping down my throat.

She just looked at me. "That's not super exciting, but that does suck. I'm glad you're feeling better," she paused, giving her attention to one of the soccer boys kicking across the field. "Anything else?"

"Well, I mean, my letter came," I said. The words came out like concrete. They weighed my jaw down to the dewy grass.

"Wait. Did you get in?" she gasped. She sat up on her knees.

I said nothing and tried to look anywhere but toward her quickly sinking face.

"Oh…" she whispered. She didn't need me to tell her. She thought about it a second more and then set her notebook down. She watched me as I watched the grass. Our feet had stamped two parallel paths into the soccer field leading from the school doors to where we sat. The grass had slowly been rising back to its tall stance where our footprints had been.

Elena inched forward on her knees to hug me. Her bare arms stuck to mine and she smelled just like I knew she would, like lavender with a hint of underground bars, smoke and whiskey. A curl brushed against my forehead. She let go, settling back into the grass.

"Come with me," she said.

I looked up and raised an eyebrow. "Where? Right now?" I asked.

"No, silly. You can join me and the guys on the tour," she continued.

"Elena, no," I replied. I couldn't just tag along like a dead leaf stuck to the tire of their tour van.

"Why not?" she asked, pouting her lips. She picked her notebook up and set it back in her lap.

"Because…what would I do? I'm not in the band." I started doodling purple stars in the corners of my notebook again. "Plus, what about my dad? I don't want to leave him alone all summer."

"You can write. And help us out with anything we need on the trip, like setting up for shows and grabbing us food and drinks between sets and stuff. You'd be like our personal assistant but then you'd also get to party with us after too…" She paused, starting to fantasize. Then she added, "And your dad will be fine. He's practically alone all the time anyway because he stays out in that garden. He'd probably love the idea of you traveling since that's something he and your mom always wanted to do." After sending a reassuring smile my way, Elena paused for a moment and watched the soccer boys. Then she let out a soft laugh and said, "You can help me make sure the guys don't get into any trouble too."

"That sounds like a fun job," I answered sarcastically.

"Well, it'd be better than sitting at home right?" She watched me for a couple more seconds, and then started to pay more attention to her notebook again. I did

the same and started to contemplate her offer.

Chapter 4

The rest of the school year went by fast, but each day felt like a whole week on their own. Every second not spent focusing on homework or talking on the phone with Elena was spent thinking about that stupid letter. I wanted to go with Elena so badly, but I needed some sort of purpose. If I didn't have one, I would just think about all of the things I could do at home: making sure my dad was alright, keeping the house clean, working at the library to help Dad with groceries. Then again, if I wasn't at home, he would only need to buy half the groceries.

The idea of being home felt safe and warm, but also lonely, especially now that my dad felt like only half a person after my mom left. I knew deep down that I'd have more opportunities on the road. There was something holding me back, though. Part of me convinced myself that my mom was that something. Like somehow, her spirit was tying my arms to my bedposts and whispering in my ear to stay with her forever. But I know my mom…at least, the mom I knew before baby Orion died, would've wanted me to leave. She would have wanted me to get out of Indiana as soon as I could. But she'd also want me to do something important with my life.

I tried to keep myself busy as long as possible, keeping my mind off of everything. I worked extremely hard on my homework. Every paper assigned would be finished and three pages longer than needed because it was something else I could focus on. When I had too much to do, I couldn't feel sad.

About a month before finals came prom. I planned on going solo, with Elena and Jack as backup, but Jack told Wes on a whim and he said he would join too. They all kept it a secret until they were already on their way to my house. I would have been too nervous if I had known before. I had never hung out with just Wes before. Even when I hung out with the entire band all together, they never left just him and I alone.

I stood in my room staring at my dress in the mirror and doing minor touch ups to my makeup and hair. My dress had a high-neckline and sheer mesh panels above my chest and across my stomach. The bottom was all black tulle and flowed behind me when I walked. On my face, I winged out the perfect cat eye look and slapped on some dark purple lipstick. I had straightened my hair and put a black beaded clip behind one of my ears as my only accessory. At exactly five o'clock, Elena walked in the front door and yelled for me. I put on one last swipe of lipstick, grabbed my purse, and headed toward her.

Outside on the porch, my dad took pictures of us in front of one of the giant pine trees in our front yard. I stood next to Wes who showed off a pearly smile. His long hair curled down his forehead. He wore a white button down shirt, black slacks, black shoes, and coincidentally, a purple bowtie that matched my lipstick.

Elena and Jack posed next to us. Elena wore her hair up in a curly bun with little ringlets framing her face and a long red silk gown that plunged deep in the front, almost to her belly button. Jack had his hair slicked back and wore a simple all black tux and a red bowtie. After pictures, Elena, Jack, and Wes started to get into the car and I walked to my dad. He handed me my phone back.

"I hopefully got some good ones," he said.

I nodded and placed my phone into my black faux fur clutch.

"You look great. I wish she could have been here to see you," he said.

I looked up at him quickly. He couldn't look at my eyes but there was a small smile on his face. It was like one of those smiles when you've been crying for a while and then your best friend tells you a joke to make you laugh.

"Me too, Dad," I said. I walked to him and wrapped my arms around his shoulders and he squeezed back. I drew in a deep breath and could smell the forest and ground coffee on his neck.

I pulled back, squeezed his shoulders with my hands as a goodbye, and walked to the car. He slowly made his way to the front steps and sat down, watching us drive away.

On the way to dinner at the Mayberry Cafe, we jammed to a Hey Violet album on the highest volume. Then we headed over to the event center where they had prom every year. The building looked like a small factory from the outside but a sign by the door said, "Danville Prom, Inside to the Left." We followed the sign's directions, through the automated glass doors and down the 90s printed carpeted hallway toward a dark room with blaring pop music.

Elena leaned over to me once we all stopped inside the door and said, "It's a little better than I expected, I guess."

I nodded and studied the room. The committee decided on an "Enchanted Tea Party" theme and for the most part, they pulled it off. It was pretty dark in the room, but bright white and pink lights roamed the room from a setup near the front. White, pink, and green balloons bounced around the ceiling. Fake moss spotted with pink flowers and fairy lights hung around the walls and pillars. A DJ who looked around forty stood on the stage, moving from side to side behind his laptop. In front of the stage was a dance floor and every junior and senior from our school dancing or mingling in the center wearing brightly colored gowns and tuxes. Tables lined the dance floor on both sides. They each held a pink and white checkered tablecloth and a few people, drinking punch or soda from little clear plastic cups.

To our right was the "bar" which only had the options of non-alcoholic pink punch, pink lemonade, and Sprite. We all walked over and got three Sprites and walked to a table crammed into a corner of the room.

"Don't worry, I brought something else to drink," Wes said over the music.

He pulled out a flask from his jacket and poured vodka into all three of our drinks. Elena and I laughed and clinked our cups together. Jack glared at Wes for a second and then gave in, letting Wes pour a little into his cup too.

After that, the night was pretty uneventful. Robert, Mike, and Lexi from gym danced in a group with some of their other friends so we avoided them at all costs. A guy in Elena's AP biology class came over to talk to her and then asked me to dance. I politely turned him down and he took it well, smiling and walking straight to another group of girls to ask one of them. Elena laughed, shook her head, and then grabbed Jack and I's hands and dragged us to the edge of the dance floor. Wes trailed behind. We all danced together, Elena and I holding hands most of the time. Wes kept pulling out these strange but cool dance moves that I had never seen before and Jack knew every word of every song that played, even genres I had no idea he liked. I realized that this could be how much fun I'd have on tour with them. I thought about it for a full song and then tried focusing on other things instead.

Tonight was not about figuring out my life. I needed to let go.

The rest of the night, we danced, refilled our drinks a few times (Jack stopped before us so he could drive later), and requested songs that nobody else in the room probably knew. At the end of the night, Jack drove us home and Elena and I cuddled in the backseat while he sang along to an album I hadn't heard before. Wes sat in the front seat, scrolling through the pictures we had all taken that night. After pulling into my driveway, I opened the door and gave Elena a sloppy kiss on the cheek. The ground moved under my feet as I walked and I could hear the gravel extra clearly.

"Seren!"

I turned around. Wes hung out the front window.

"I know we didn't get to dance together tonight. But, raincheck?" he asked. The smirk on his face grew with every second I didn't reply.

After thinking it through, I just nodded. Stumbling over myself as I tried to twirl back into the direction I was walking.

"I had a good time!" he yelled once I got to my front steps.

"Me too!" I yelled back. I didn't give him the satisfaction of turning back around as I answered.

Once inside, I floated through the hallway to my bedroom holding my heels. I threw them into my closet, slipped off my dress, and passed out immediately in my bed.

Finals came next. I aced my film test, my English essay, and my art project, and received nothing over a C in everything else. My dad asked how they went and I said, "Fine," and he nodded and said he was proud of me. My

mom would have given me a stern look and pulled all of
her old history and math textbooks out and sat me down for
a couple hours. She would've made sure I knew what I
needed to know, even if I couldn't bring up my grades. My
dad just seemed content that I had passed, or that I was at
least content with myself enough that I didn't need to tell
him if I passed or failed.

A couple weeks after that came graduation. One
diploma for Seren E. Moore. One diploma for Elena A.
Cipriani. My dad had a work meeting but Vivian and Gio
waved and hollered just as much for me as they did for
their own daughter. Jack, Wes, and Munro all did the same.
Although I knew they had come to support their band mate,
they still made it feel like they were there for me too. I
smiled widely for all of them as I grabbed my diploma and
shook my principal's hand because I was happy I at least
had them watching over me. Afterward, Elena and I took
pictures in our caps and gowns, including one from outside

in the parking lot flipping off the high school. Then we went our separate ways.

I made myself a cup of tea at home. All the rooms were dark, only a slight light coming in through the sliding doors that led to the garden. I sat on the couch, sipping my tea, and just stared at my diploma. A sad nostalgic feeling fluttered through my stomach, followed by an audible sigh of relief that lifted my shoulders out of a tense hold, and finally, a slight panic shocking feeling throughout my chest.

What's next, Seren?

I stayed at Elena's the next night. I woke up in Elena's bed that morning and stretched my arm out, reaching for her presence but there was nothing. She was already up. I slowly rolled my body over, wrapped up in her pink cotton sheets and the heavy quilt her grandmother made her. The clock on the wall said 10:45 AM.

I lifted my legs out of the bed and settled my feet into the plush carpet. I wiggled my toes, reached my arms above my head, and took a deep breath in. My arms floated down as I let the air out in a big sigh.

After pulling sweats on over my boy shorts, I made my way out into the kitchen where Elena and Vivian flipped pancakes. Gio sat at the table reading a cycling magazine.

"Ah, good morning, Little Star." Vivian turned, giving me a grin. Her straight black hair was pulled up into a long ponytail with a scrunchy, and she wore her usual fluffy peach robe.

"Good morning," I replied, sitting next to Gio at the table.

"You can tell her you're too old for that nickname anytime now," said Gio. He nudged me in the arm and winked. He still looked like he could be a high schooler: no wrinkles, bright green eyes, a full head of thick, dark curls. He wore a matching green flannel pajama set.

Vivian walked over with a platter of pancakes in one hand and syrup in the other, and set them both on the table. Elena grabbed peanut butter from a cabinet and handed it to me. I unscrewed the lid. Vivian sat next to me, which left the seat across from me open for Elena. Sitting between her parents, it was obvious she was the perfect mixture of them both. Black hair and tan skin like Vivian, who was half-Egyptian and half-Jamaican. Heavy curls and olive eyes like Gio, whose mother and father moved to the United States from Italy when he was five.

I felt like the opposite of them all. Short white hair and pale pink skin with dark green-brown eyes that seemed a little too harsh for my own face. Like Vivian told me when I was little, I was the brightest star in the middle of their dark universe. No matter our looks, they made me feel more at home than I felt anywhere else.

"We're going shopping for Lena's trip later today. Are you joining us?" Vivian poured maple syrup out of a white ceramic jar onto her plate as Amy Winehouse played softly from the radio on the counter.

"Yeah, sure," I said. I spread peanut butter onto the top pancake, taking as long as I could.

"I definitely need a new suitcase. That old polka-dotted one's wheel is broken," Elena said to her mom. Vivian passed her the syrup. She nodded.

"I'll add it to the list. Seren, do you need anything for this summer?" Vivian asked. I watched the syrup drip off the knife as she lifted it and I nodded absentmindedly. "Have you thought of a new plan yet?"

I shook my head and avoided eye contact.

"Have you told your dad?"

Again, I gave her nothing. I felt bad. I hated disappointing her.

"You know, Mom...I've been trying to get Seren to join us on tour," said Elena.

Vivian looked at me, one questioning eyebrow raising.

"I said I'd think about it," I said, laughing at Elena wiggling with excitement in her seat.

"She says she'll have too much to do…working at the library," Elena groaned. "But the guys and I really want her to come."

"And helping my dad out." I paused. "Wait…the guys want me to come?" I asked. I set my knife down on a napkin on the table. Gio smirked next to me.

"Yeah…mostly Wes. He thinks you're cool," she grinned. Elena stared at me as if she were trying to talk telepathically.

"Well…maybe. I told you. I need to figure it out," I said.

"There's nothing to figure out," Elena groaned. "Come on the tour. Write. Save me from being the only girl in our crowded van. Figure it out on the road."

I glared at her. "Maybe."

She shook her head and started eating her pancakes. Vivian and Gio started a new conversation about something unrelated. I ate my pancakes, blocking out the rest of the table for the entirety of breakfast.

Near the end of the meal, I remembered it was Sunday and I actually had a good reason to leave Elena and her family's questions behind for the day: I had to work today.

At two o'clock I drove myself the few miles to the library, a two-story concrete slab squared in by four one-way roads and a few community planted trees. I swung my body out of my car, feeling the sun on my bare legs before I stood. My grey tank dress swished around my body as I grabbed my backpack out of the backseat. I threw it over my shoulder as I made my way to the front door.

Inside, the air felt thick in my lungs. It wasn't a suffocating thickness, but more like a comforting heavy blanket on a chilly summer night. The entrance smelled like freshly cut grass.

"Afternoon, Seren," whispered Helen from her perch at the front desk. She always seemed to whisper, even when no one else around her did. Her hair was held high in a curly bun with a red and orange headscarf and her thick, teal glasses encompassed the entirety of the top half of her face.

"Hello, Helen," I replied. I made my way around the desk and into the back office. "Are there books to shelve from the morning?" I asked through the doorway as I set my backpack next to everyone else's purses and lunchboxes.

"Two whole carts," Helen said.

"I'll start there, then," I said. Helen watched absentmindedly as I made my way over to one of the big rolling books carts. I started by organizing them by category: fiction, non-fiction, children's, etc. After that, I focused on each section and shifted them around until they were in order by either the authors' last names or the

Dewey Decimal number. Once I finished, I started rolling it around to each section.

The library seemed pretty empty, not unusual. An older man, a regular named Erwin, sat in a window seat reading a historical novel about WWII. His usual reads were about Vietnam, but even when he strayed, it was never too far from the general war category. At a table in the back corner behind the young adult fiction sat a girl from my high school that I recognized, but couldn't remember her name. She would be a sophomore next year. Her hair was straight and black as coal and swished down to her hips as she walked. I always admired her hair in the hallways as I passed her. Mine seemed to crimp on its own, which is why I usually keep it short. She had her laptop out, headphones in, and an AP biology textbook opened to a page near the end.

I turned the corner and stopped at the biography section, where I took the first three books off the rack and started to put them back into their designated slots. They slid in between their book companions like the perfect

engagement ring on a finger. I held the last book in my

hands and glanced through its empty space on the shelf.

Row on row of books of all sizes and colors and stories

expanded behind it through the room. And as I stared

through the gap, I swore I felt someone's eyes on me too.

A chill rose through my body and I looked down at my

arms. My ice blonde hair rose along with tiny goosebumps.

I slid the last book into its spot and walked the rack quickly

out into the open, looking over my shoulder a couple times

for good measure.

There wasn't anyone or anything else in the library

other than Helen, Erwin, and the girl from my high school.

Maybe I really do need to get out of here.

Two weeks later, Elena left. She drove by my

house to say goodbye before going on to Jack's apartment

downtown. I trudged outside in a big black sweater, yoga

pants, and bare feet.

"Why are you wearing that?" Elena asked, stepping out of her car in running shorts, a tank, and flip-flops. Her hair had been pulled up in a bun in a big scrunchie. "It's like eighty degrees and it's only ten."

"You know Dad likes the house cold," I answered. I smiled, curling my hands into my sweater and pulling on the sleeves. "You're leaving me."

"I am. But you could have come," she said. She nudged my leg with her foot, jingling her car keys in one hand. "And I'm not leaving forever, obviously."

I nodded and went in for a hug. She pulled away and laughed again. "Yeah, no. Too hot," she laughed. She pulled at the front of my sweater.

"Tell Wes I'm sorry," I said.

Elena smirked. "Oh, I will. He'll just be absolutely devastated."

I smiled widely. "Good."

"I should probably go now. I told Jack I'd be there in half an hour." She looked down at her keys, a curl falling gently onto her sunny golden forehead.

"Text me, love you?" I held my hand out for her.

"Text me. Love you always," she answered. She took my hand, gave it a squeeze, and let go, walking backwards to her car.

I walked back to the concrete step before the front door, watching my feet to miss any sharp pieces of rock. I sat down and watched Elena step into her car. She started the engine. As she backed out, she waved frantically through the window and I could tell even from far away that her eyes were tearing up. I pulled my knees up to my chest and waved with my sweater-covered hand. Once she was out of sight, I drew my hands into fists and rubbed my closed eyelids until I saw flecks of light bouncing around in my head. I opened my eyes again and the flecks continued, fluttering around the air in front of me. Once I saw clearly again, the car was gone and the tires crunching

on the gravel had stopped. She was gone.

Chapter 5

After Elena left, I fell face first into my comforter with open arms. The covers sunk with my body and surrounded me. I enjoyed the tight quarters for a while until I fell asleep and almost accidentally suffocated. When I woke up, I panicked. Not only did I feel like the air was being dragged out of my body but the space I resided in felt wrong. It was like I was stuck inside a rolling cloud. Everything in my head felt foggy and obscured. My room wasn't my room anymore. This place wasn't my house.

I got up and changed. I didn't want the sweater anymore. Even though the house was under sixty degrees, my skin stuck to the fabric. I threw on an old Aerosmith shirt and jean shorts, and threw my hair up into a tiny messy bun. Makeup still smeared under my eyes from the day before, and I wiped as much away as I could with my bare hands. I still looked like I'd been dead for a few hours.

I tried cleaning my room. I picked up clothes off the floor, worn oversized band tees, ripped jeans, mountains of socks, throwing them into my overflowing dirty clothes basket across the room. I made my bed. I moved the empty soda cans and water bottles off of every surface to the kitchen trash. Then my room was clean. I tried writing, but when I sat down at my laptop the screen looked distorted and my fingers wouldn't move on the keyboard. I grabbed a notebook but the pages felt too frail, like they'd disintegrate under a pen. For an hour, I tried different things to make myself feel normal again. Nothing worked.

My feet led me outside again. I didn't need another swim, though. Maybe just some fresh air this time. I closed the sliding door behind me and sat down on the porch. The garden stood only a few feet away but vines and short trees blocked my view. I watched the clouds roll across the gray sky.

I could hear the train from across town. Its wheels sounded like a slow thunder. My legs folded up into my chest and I breathed in the air, sweet and warm, like breakfast in the morning. The train flowed with the pattern of my heart beat and I felt myself grounding to the earth, or in this case, the wooden porch. My bare feet pressed hard against the planks.

A gust of wind rushed between the house and the garden and it blew little yellow honeysuckle flowers onto the porch. I picked one up and pulled off the stem. A clear nectar pearled up and I licked it off. My mom and I used to pull them off a few days after they bloomed, when they started to smell the best, and would taste the sweetest honey, starting off the hot summer. They tasted how they smelled, light and fresh and sugary.

I set the flower trumpet back on the porch and turned around to look in the glass doors. Through the glass was an eerie darkness. Lines of black and gray and little gleams of light from the sky swirled around behind the door, like a never-ending whirlpool.

I stood and walked over to the garden, under the vine archway and into the little canopy my dad built years ago. He sat there in his armchair. His hair was messy, shirt unbuttoned a couple notches, and dark stubble grew into a short beard across his gentle cheeks. He wrote in a notebook, scribbling out some parts and circling others.

"Hey, Dad… I think I'm leaving," I stated.

He looked up from his notebook over his glasses.

"I mean, uh, I'm gonna go with Elena and the band on tour…" I started. "I think I told you they invited me, right?"

He set his pencil down. "Oh, right. Just for the summer?" he asked.

I nodded and winced inside.

He looked around the garden. Then he shook his head slightly and looked back up at me. "Do you need anything? There's a big suitcase in the bottom of the towel closet if you want to use it." His eyes were only half open, like he was staring into the sun.

"Thanks, Dad. That should be all I need," I replied.

"Are you leaving right now?" he asked.

"Yeah. I'm meeting Elena at her boyfriend's," I said.

We both stayed silent for a moment. I shuffled and my arm rustled the honeysuckle bush next to me.

"Okay. Well, have fun. Be safe. Those groupies can be crazy." He forced a smile.

"I will," I assured. I turned to walk away, smelling the sweet honeysuckle bushes lining the walkway. I quickly turned back around and stuck my head around the bushes. "You'll be okay, right?" I asked.

"Of course. Your dad's been a big adult for quite a while now, honey," he assured. He sent me a soft smile this time, an understanding one.

I started to walk off again and stopped just for another moment, just to hear him start writing again.

"I love you, Seren," he said, instead.

I stopped. A breeze blew a few strands of hair across my face. Honeysuckle.

I heard him start to write again.

"I love you too, Dad." I walked off to the house without looking back.

I dragged the musty suitcase out of the bottom of the towel closet and took it to my room. I lifted it up and tossed it onto my bed. After running around my room for an hour, I had thrown in a few t-shirts, a sweatshirt, a few pairs of shorts, a couple dresses, some pajamas, socks, a couple pairs of shoes, and all of my makeup and toiletries. I looked around my room for anything else I might need. *Norwegian Wood* sat on my desk. I grabbed it and tossed it in and then struggled to zip it closed.

In the living room, I stopped. The room was dark and the light from outside shined through the back sliding doors. I could barely see the edge of the garden from where I stood. I shook my head and kept going.

I dragged the suitcase through the gravel driveway and lifted it into the trunk of my car. I slammed it shut, then walked to the driver's side door. My fingers trembled as I opened it. I tossed my backpack into the passenger's seat and got in. I closed the door.

I wasn't actually joining the band, so where was I going?

I couldn't go to my grandma's in Indy because she would instantly tell Dad and he'd get mad that I lied to him. I didn't really have other friends.

I couldn't decide where to go so I just started the engine. It cracked in the heat. I rolled the windows down and backed out the driveway, listening to the gravel crunch and fly out from the tires. On the road, I turned the radio on and as I shuffled through, Stevie Nicks started singing the chorus of "Landslide." I stayed on that station and kept my eyes on the white dashes flying by on the asphalt. For a while, the radio kept me occupied. I didn't think about anything.

About three hours in, I had driven south and made it to Evansville, almost to the border of Kentucky. It was starting to get dark. All of the stations I liked were out of range now, so I switched to an old Bob Dylan CD that had been lying on the floor of the passenger side. Lights and signs passed by, but I tried to pay no attention. I just kept going.

After a couple more hours, I had to stop and get gas. I pulled off a backroad past the Cumberland City exit. At the station, I shivered outside the car from the cool summer air. I wrapped my arms around myself and waited for the tank to fill. There was nothing else around, just the station and the road. Bright yellow circles glowed from the direction I came. A truck, jacked up at least two feet, maybe more, drove up to the other fill station. I pulled up on the lever to let it fall and stop the flow of gasoline.

While I put the dispenser back into its slot, three guys

around my age stepped out of the truck. All three wore dirt-

covered, cut-off tanks, jeans with big belt buckles, and

work boots. The one wearing a cowboy hat walked straight

inside the station.

The tallest one with reddish hair stood by the

filling station while the other, a short boy with a flying

American flag tattoo on his shoulder hopped up into the

back of the truck. The tires bounced and he wobbled and

then sat down on the edge.

I walked around to the trunk of my car, trying to

avoid any real eye contact. I popped it and pulled my

suitcase further to me. After unzipping it, I searched for a

sweatshirt.

The redhead whistled.

I pretended to not hear it and lifted my school's

senior hoodie out of my suitcase. I pulled it over my t-shirt.

He whistled again, this time much louder, and the boy in the bed started to laugh.

"I'm not a fucking pet." I kept the comment under my breath.

"What was that, sweet thing?" the redhead called.

I walked around to the driver's door as they laughed with each other and watched. I got in and slammed the door as hard as I could, locking the doors after. I sped away, lifting my middle finger to the window as I left them behind.

Half an hour later, I felt my heart racing from thinking about the gas station incident so I stopped driving. Right outside of Yellow Creek, Tennessee, a little motel with pink doors and flower beds in every window called to me. I parked and walked inside the front office. I paid for just one night with my library desk money and my fake ID, took my key, and lugged my suitcase out of my car. I rolled the suitcase to room four and unlocked the door.

Stars in the Honey

The inside definitely wasn't as appealing as the outside, but it would do. It had one queen sized bed, a desk, a small dresser, and a small bathroom in the back. Everything was either an off-white color or some kind of wood. I lifted my suitcase up onto the desk and unzipped it. After stepping out of my jean shorts, I pulled on black leggings. I went through my usual night routine, washing my face, brushing my teeth, and then stretching in some resting yoga poses.

I didn't bring my mat so I opted for the bed since the carpet seemed questionable. My body sunk into the layers of blankets. My forehead rested on the bed, nose close to my knees. I let my shoulders fall loosely downward and I felt the stretch in the muscles after driving for so long. I pulled a long breath into my lungs.

The bedspread smelled slightly of smoke, and I started to miss Elena. It hadn't even been twenty-four hours yet, but I felt the weight of knowing I'd have to wait months to see her again. I let the breath out and I fell limply to the side. I kept my face close to the bedspread. Another deep breath. More smoke.

I missed her.

I got up and grabbed my phone off the desk, then sat back down on the bed. I had one text from her: "Miss you. Hope you're eating a ton of peanut butter pancakes tomorrow morning for me."

I smiled, shuffling my phone around in my hands. After a moment, I set it down on the bed and got up. In the bathroom, I turned the shower on and let it heat up until steam billowed out of the doorway. I stripped down and stepped in. I tried my best not to feel like Marion Crane in *Psycho*. Then again, I don't think I'd ever felt that happy taking a shower.

I closed my eyes and took a breath in. Steam filled my sinuses. Water plummeted from the faucet like hot needles. They pulsed against my shoulders, massaging deep toward my muscles and veins. I tried to push all thoughts out of my mind. I focused on the droplets of water falling from my forehead, to my lips, down my neck, to my chest. Some ran quickly, some slow. A foggy steam surrounded my body and I moved through it, feeling the dense air cling to my skin.

I opened my eyes. My skin turned patchy and red. I poured a dot of shampoo into my hand and kneaded it into my hair. I rinsed and did the same with conditioner. I took the packaged soap bar and opened it, rubbing it into my skin until I felt clean. After one last rinse, I turned off the shower and stepped out. The tile was slick under my feet.

In the next room, my phone started to ring. I grabbed a towel off the rack on the wall and wrapped it around me. On the bed, my phone buzzed and "Lena" flashed on the screen. I ran over and picked it up, putting the phone up to my wet hair. I maneuvered it around to my ear.

"Elena?" I answered.

"Seren? You read my text and didn't respond," she said.

I stayed silent.

"Uh, why? We said, 'Text me, love you.' That means you have to text back," she continued. Her voice sounded strained on the other side and I couldn't help but laugh a little.

"I'm sorry. I, uh, really needed a shower," I explained.

"I guess that's okay. Jack, stop, I'm talking to Seren." She paused and I heard her floaty laugh from miles away. "Wes says hi."

"Hi, Wes." I rolled my eyes to myself. "And hi Jack and Munro too. Can't leave them out."

Elena said something to the guys again and then to me, "So, Best Friend, what all did you do today?"

I paused, considering my options. I could tell her everything was fine and continue on my destination-less journey and keep "figuring things out" or I could just give in to her joining-the-band idea.

I opted for neither right away and instead said, "I went location scouting."

"Location scouting? Like for a script idea?" she asked.

"Uh, yeah. But then I got hit on by these weird cowboys at a gas station, so it kind of failed," I said, trying to keep it vague.

"Which gas station? That one over by Dairy Queen? That's a gross one, you know that."

"No, no. Uh…I'm not home," I said, wincing, waiting for the harsh voice I knew would come across that phone speaker.

"What the hell, Seren. Where are you? It's one in the morning. You can't just be out random places —" Elena started.

"Lena, calm down. I'm at a motel. I'm fine," I assured her.

"Okay, honestly though, motels aren't much better. Where is this motel?" she asked.

"Um…" I started.

"Seren, seriously. Where are you?" she asked. Apparently, I had taken too long to answer.

"Somewhere in Tennessee," I said quietly.

I heard her sigh deeply and say, "I don't care why you're really there but my best friend is not staying in motels for the summer."

There was a long pause. I didn't know what to say. I didn't want to tell her that I couldn't stay at home because I felt trapped by my mother's ghost and my father's almost-lifeless body. I didn't want to tell her that I felt like a burden following her everywhere I go. I didn't want to tell her that I felt completely worthless after receiving the rejection letter. I couldn't tell the truth, so what was I supposed to say?

"I, uh…" I started but she cut me off.

"Seren, please, please join us. You can scout locations as we go. You can write screenplays the entire time. Please?" Elena pleaded.

I laid back onto the bed. I wanted to give in so badly. I wanted to travel and go to Elena's shows and eat take-out and hotel breakfasts every morning. I wanted to forget about my mom. Just for a little while.

"You sure no one will mind?" I asked. I was caving. It was over. The second I asked that question, the second I thought I might just do it, I knew I would.

"They definitely won't. I told you, the guys have practically been begging." A pause. Then to one of the guys: "Yes, you have and you know it."

"Okay."

She pulled a breath in quickly. "Really? You really want to come?"

"Yes." Fuck.

There was no turning back now. "Oh my god, yes! Where are you?" Elena asked.

"Somewhere outside Yellow Creek, Tennessee."

"Uh…okay. Cool place?" I heard her tapping on her phone, probably looking up where I was exactly.

"We're in Ashland City right now, and then we have to be in Nashville around four o'clock in the afternoon tomorrow. So you're like only an hour away. You can meet us here in the morning and leave your car with Jack's friend that we're staying with."

"Yeah, okay. I can do that."

"Please be safe, Seren. Don't turn into a Marion Crane." She knew how my brain worked too well sometimes.

"Promise," I replied.

"Okay. Text me, love you," she said.

"Text me, love you. I'll see you in the morning," I answered.

She hung up. I set my phone down next to me on the bed. I covered my face with my hands and groaned.

After a few panicking thoughts, I got up and wrapped the towel around my hair instead of my body. I threw on underwear and a big night shirt from my suitcase. Then I walked to the front door and made sure it was locked. Growing more paranoid, I checked all of the walls

for any holes and around the room for anything else

suspicious. I found nothing except an odd green stain near

the window and a one dollar bill inside the nightstand

Bible. Finally, I laid in bed, hair still in my towel and fell

asleep nestled under the layers of sheets and fleece

blankets.

Chapter 6

At seven-thirty A.M. I woke up with the sunlight. I quickly changed into black cut-off shorts and a green t-shirt that read "Let the Shenanigans Begin." Appropriate.

I packed everything up again, slipped my flip-flops back on, and threw my hair back up in a bun since sleeping with it in a towel did it no justice. Some of the shorter pieces stuck out around my forehead and ears.

I threw my suitcase into the backseat of my car. In the office, I turned my key in and said thank you to the nice reception lady. My car rumbled to life and I sped out onto the road. Everything flew by and around nine in the morning, I was in Ashland City.

As I drove, the houses became closer together and eventually, each house barely had a few feet of yard around them before the next one began. This wasn't surprising. I had seen many a subdivision before in Indiana. But as I continued, I realized I had rarely been out of Indiana at all. There was that one trip in fifth grade with my school to Washington D.C., and that time my parents took me to see a strange version of Julius Caesar on stage in Chicago. But other than that, my feet had never reached another state's soil. I had never driven down backroads in another state, never seen their subdivisions. Although now, looking at one slowly passing me by, it didn't seem like quite as big of a deal. It looked familiar.

The rows and rows of brick and bold red doors blurred outside my car window until finally, my GPS told me that the destination would be after my next turn. I drove down a short street ending in a cul-de-sac and parked along the side of the huge asphalt circle. After turning the key and listening to the engine quickly die, I saw Elena bounding out the door of a very plain looking brick house. This one didn't even have a red door.

I had texted Elena all morning, giving her updates on where I was and how long I would be and apparently, she had been waiting. She wore a black and white striped t-shirt dress with bare feet. Her hair floated around her head as she ran down the front yard to my car.

I opened the door. "Lena!" My heart pounded as she neared me.

Her arms wrapped around my neck and her breath landed heavily on my cheek. "I can't believe you're here," she said, pulling away and smiling wildly. "This is gonna be fun."

I gave her a look of excited panic and then walked around to the trunk. I grabbed my suitcase and hauled it up to the house with Elena bouncing by my side.

"This is Ethan's house. He's a friend of Jack's. We're using Ethan's van for the tour and leaving him Jack's car. He's not home though so you might not even meet him."

"That's okay." I lifted the suitcase up the three concrete steps to the front door.

Elena opened it for me. "Just set your suitcase there." She pointed to a spot where everyone's shoes laid. I set it down and slipped off my flip-flops into the pile.

In the living room, Jack laid on a puffy gray couch in plaid red pajama pants and a black tank top. The room felt cozy, surrounded in all different shades of white, gray, and navy. Every surface, besides the walls, was made of a comforting fabric: corduroy, faux fur, suede. Even the TV sat on its own navy blue rug that covered the entirety of the table holding it up.

"Hey, Jack." I stepped onto the plush smoke-gray carpet and held my arms out.

"Seren! Hey! I'm so glad you decided to come." He stood up and engulfed me. Even at 5'9", he made me feel short. I couldn't imagine how Elena felt, being four inches shorter than me. As he let go he said, "Wes is making breakfast in the kitchen if you want anything."

I gave Elena a look and she reciprocated.

"I'm okay. I had some real good gas station food on the way over," I said.

Jack grinned and made his way to an archway that seemed like it would lead to the kitchen.

"I think Munro is still sleeping, but he should be up soon." Elena started walking toward the kitchen too. She looked back at me. "I don't know about you, but I'd rather have Wes' scrambled eggs over gas station food any day."

I rolled my eyes at her, but followed. Through the archway, bacon, eggs, and toast filled the countertops on ceramic plates. Wes stood in front of the stove, his hair pulled back out of his face with a running headband. He wore basketball shorts and no shirt, showing off the tattoos covering his back. A magnolia branch covered one of his shoulders. He turned around with a pan to shovel more eggs onto another plate. A wide grin spread across his face, one side reaching up a little higher than the other. The green in his eyes seemed to swirl around as I looked in them.

"Seren…" His eyes searched around my face and landed on my own eyes again. "Eggs?" He smirked and took a couple steps toward me.

Suddenly, it was a little harder to breathe. "Uh, yes, please. No bacon though."

I looked over at Elena who had the most mischievous grin on her face. Wes walked toward me. I turned so he could squeeze by to the counter. His bare arm brushed mine and instantly I felt scorched, like his skin was a wildfire.

"Alright. These plates are your's and Munro's then." He looked at me. He liked eye contact. "No bacon."

I looked anywhere but his eyes now. And it wasn't very hard once Munro walked in.

"Hey, Seren." He plodded in, rubbing one dark eye under his clear glasses. He wore sweatpants and a tie-dye Nirvana t-shirt. His hair stuck up in wavy pieces.

"Hi, Munro," I replied.

"I'm glad you've decided to join." Munro gave me a half-smile, lingering his eyes over mine, and then moved on to the plates. "No bacon?" He pointed to the two emptier plates.

"Yours and mine," I explained.

"Ah," he sighed, then picked up his plate. He shuffled through a drawer and pulled out a fork. He picked at the eggs and stuffed a bite into his mouth. After he swallowed, he asked, "What took you so long to decide to come?"

I paused before answering, looking around at everyone else who seemed to only be half-listening to our conversation. Wes was still cooking and Jack was hugging Elena from behind, whispering or nibbling her ear. "I…uh…" I started.

"Ah, no, I get it," he started, cutting me off, You're just trying to find yourself right?" He smirked and started to walk away with his plate. Then he looked back and gave a genuine smile. He walked out of the room with his food and I could hear him shuffle around in the next room and finally, turn on the TV.

I turned and rested my elbows back onto the counter. Wes glanced over at me with a pale look. He finished making his last batch of bacon, turned to sloppily plop the strips onto a couple of the plates, and then started to do the dishes haphazardly.

Elena lifted her eyebrow at me and I shrugged.

"So when are we leaving?" I asked, straining my voice over the rattlings pans and rushing water.

"In about two hours, I think," Elena responded.

I nodded in return.

Jack grabbed his plate from the counter and gestured that we should follow. Elena and I grabbed our plates too and made our way behind Jack into the living room.

Chapter 7

Two and a half hours later, the band was packed and ready to go, and we headed toward Nashville in Jack's friend's van. It was a dark maroon with mustard-colored accents. There were three rows of seating and a big trunk for most of the equipment. Their manager, Patrick (Munro's uncle), would take the rest of the equipment around in his own car. The band's driver, Frank, sat in the front of the van and waited for us to pack everything in. Frank was Patrick's friend and an unmarried, college professor so he got the summers free and decided it'd be fun to follow a band around for his vacation. And Patrick agreed it would be nice having a friend to hang out with while as of us "young-ins," as he called us, went out and had fun.

Jack and Elena climbed into the back row of seats and spread themselves out to nap. Wes hopped into the middle row without a thought and Munro and I looked at each other. "I'll take the front. It's pretty crowded with three," he said. He climbed into the front row and gave a quick nod to Frank. I climbed in after Wes and set my bag in between us. Wes quickly pulled out his laptop and set it on his legs.

"I'm trying out songwriting. Elena usually does it, as you probably already know," he started, glancing back at Elena who smiled widely. "But I thought I'd try and help out a little."

"I'm sure whatever you write will be great," said Elena. I nodded to agree.

Wes grinned and stuck his earbuds in, starting to write.

Munro stuck a disc in the van's CD player, and I immediately recognized it as Jimmy Eat World's "Bleed American." He stared out the window as Frank started driving away. We passed suburban house after suburban house again, and I had to turn away from the window. I pulled *Norwegian Wood* out of my bag and started to read. Although I could see Munro tapping his fingers against the window sill in front of me and hear Wes' keyboard clicking away, I became immersed in Murakami's words quickly.

I stopped on page 25 after reading, "Death exists, not as the opposite but as a part of life."

When I looked up, a sign on the side of the road indicated we'd be in Nashville in just six miles. Elena and Jack had fallen asleep behind me. Wes had given up on writing and started watching *Silver Linings Playbook* downloaded on his laptop. Munro still stared out the window. Now, I tried keeping my focus outside my window so I wouldn't notice the back of Munro's neck tightening every time he moved or the way his eyes looked dark and heavy in his window's reflection.

Instead, I watched the other cars pass by. After about ten more minutes we were stopped in front of our hotel. Frank got out first and started unloading suitcases from the back. Wes was next, packing up his laptop, hopping out of the van, and practically running around to the back to help Frank. Munro and I grabbed our stuff slower and trudged around to the back, stretching our legs out.

Elena and Jack stayed inside for a bit and folded up the blanket they had brought along. After a couple minutes they trudged out, rubbing their eyes. Elena's curls toppled over her forehead, falling out of a bun. A yawn spilled out of her mouth. In the middle of it, she strained out a, "What time is it?"

"Almost one," answered Wes. He grabbed a suitcase from Frank and started rolling it into the hotel. The rest of us grabbed as much as we could and followed suit. I stopped in front of the door and looked straight up at the very top of the hotel, reaching at least twenty floors.

Jack walked by and leaned into me. "Munro's parents are loaded. They offered to pay for our hotel rooms," he whispered, then smiled and walked in after Wes.

"They wanted to pay for more, but I stopped them at this. It's more than enough," said Munro, walking up next to me. I smiled and we walked into the hotel together.

Once Elena and Jack came in, followed by Frank, we all got our keys from the front desk. Frank walked up to his first. Then the rest of us grabbed an elevator together and rode it to the second to top floor. Room 1124. When we walked in, Jack's mouth dropped open. Elena started bouncing like she did anytime she was nervous, excited, or furious. Wes instantly ran straight inside and disappeared behind a door. Munro just stared, unbelievably.

"Dudes! This place is huge!" Wes yelled from another room. I walked toward his voice and Munro followed.

Right through the door was a small living room and kitchenette, furnished with a plush cream couch, an armchair, and a flatscreen TV. The back wall was all window, leading out to a little balcony. Off to the right side was a doorway that opened to the master bedroom which held a king sized bed, another TV, and additional door to the balcony. Jack and Elena claimed this room instantly and also discovered the nice two-sink bathroom with a jacuzzi tub and a shower. The other room was off to the left of the living room and held two queen beds and another smaller bathroom.

"I can take the couch," I said, standing in the smaller bedroom with Wes and Munro.

Munro immediately started shaking his head. "No, no, it's all good. I'll take the couch," he insisted.

"Are you sure?" I asked.

"Yeah, man. I could take it," said Wes, although he didn't sound very convincing.

"Yep. It's all mine," Munro said, already taking his bags back out into the living room.

Wes turned to me, shrugged, and then showed the biggest bright white smile. He threw his duffel bag on the bed and pulled his suitcase around to the other side. Then, he fell back onto the bed and let out a long sigh.

I did the same, throwing my bag on the bed and pulling my suitcase over to the wall on the side. Then Elena walked in to take a glance at the room.

"Oh, nice," she commented.

"What time is the concert?" I asked, sitting on the edge of the bed.

"Starts at seven and we need to get there at like five-thirty, so we'll probably leave here around five," she said. "I'm gonna go take another nap…or you know, just lay in bed with my boyfriend because here there are no parents, no rules. We can do whatever we want." She gave a quick look over to Wes, winked at me, and then danced out of the room.

I glanced over at Wes who was shuffling through his bag. "Do you need the bathroom?" I asked.

"Nope," he replied. He stuck earbuds in and started jamming to whatever song first popped up.

I grabbed my face wash out of my bag and made my way into the bathroom. After shutting the door behind me, I looked in the mirror. *I look crazy.*

My white blonde hair looked tangled and flat. Ninety percent of it wasn't even in the ponytail anymore. Mascara that I didn't get off in the motel shower was smeared under my eyes, making me look ten times more tired than I really was. I also had some mysterious stain on the collar of my t-shirt that stood out among the bleach spots that I added just a summer earlier on purpose.

I shook my head at myself and turned on the hot water, splashing it across my face. *I needed to at least look hot if I was going to be a professional band groupie.*

Around four-thirty, I was completely ready. Elena had joined too and was finishing up her makeup. I looked in the mirror again one last time and marked the immense difference from before. My hair was curled now, loose and just a little fluffy. Thick winged eyeliner framed my too-big hazel eyes and mascara-coated lashes. Elena had lent me a dress because I didn't think about packing any nice clothes when I left home. It fit a little looser around the top and a little tighter around the bottom than it did on Elena, but it still looked nice. The spaghetti-strap, leopard print dress reached my knees and flowed nicely because of its silky fabric. I layered on dainty gold necklaces.

"Girl, you look good," Elena said, taking a step back and turning to lean against the bathroom counter.

"All thanks to you," I said, swishing the bottom of the dress back and forth.

"How does my makeup look? Not too dark?" she asked, closing her eyes.

She had done a black smoky eye look with dark lipstick. "It looks good. Maybe pack a little more eyeshadow on your left eye. I think the right looks a bit darker," I said. She turned and inspected.

"I think you're right," she said, grabbing her makeup palette again.

"I'll be out in the living room. Gotta put shoes on," I said, walking out of the bathroom. I grabbed my black Dr. Martens from the wall and walked into the living room area.

"Wow," I heard as I entered the room. I looked up and Wes, Munro, and Jack all sat side-by-side on the couch, all dressed up, watching some stand-up comedian. Jack stared at Wes who was staring up at me. Munro seemed stuck in the middle but a small smirk hid between his dimples.

"You look great," Wes said.

"Oh, thanks. It's Elena's dress," I said, sitting down on the floor to put on my shoes. I made sure my legs faced away from the guy's view so there was no possible

way any of them would see up my dress.

"Thought I recognized it," said Jack. "She almost

ready?"

"I think so. Just touching up her makeup," I

replied. I slipped my shoes on and tied them up. From my

periphery, I could tell Munro was staring. When I looked

up, he turned back to the TV.

Then Elena walked out.

"Hell, yes! That's my girl," said Jack ecstatically.

He stood up and walked to her, wrapping an arm around

her waist and lightly kissing her cheek.

Elena laughed and fluffed up her hair. She wore

black pleather shorts, a sheer black long-sleeved shirt, and

chunky black heels. "You all ready to go?" she asked.

The equipment was already packed into the van

and Patrick's car (who had arrived just an hour earlier), so

all we had to do was get to the venue and unload

everything. After a half hour of Wes screaming random lyrics at the top of his lungs, Jack and Elena cracking up at him, and Munro shaking his head with the slightest smirk on his face, we arrived at a small country/folk bar.

Patrick ran inside. When he came back out, he instructed Frank to drive around to the side alley. He parked between two tall brick buildings near a plain black door. It opened and a guy wearing a plain black t-shirt and black jeans came out and gestured for us to bring everything in that way. We all got out of the van and grabbed as much equipment as we could hold at one time and went inside. The band was immediately sat down in a small side room with patchy black walls and a red pleather couch while Patrick and Frank helped the bar employees set up the equipment. I joined the band in the room after setting a speaker on the stage.

I could hear the band talking from down the hall.

"Wes, seriously?" questioned Jack. He sat on the couch next to Elena, who had one arm intertwined with his.

"What?" asked Wes. He stood at the edge of the couch with a flask.

"You said -," Jack started.

"Dude, it's fine," said Wes.

"Are you sure?" asked Munro who stood by the door, leaning against the wall, arms crossed. He continued, "You could try going on one night without it." As I entered the room, he glanced over at me. I stood against the other side of the door.

"Damn, I'm not plastered, dude. It's not that big of a deal. Can you drop it?" Wes asked. He took a swig. When he swallowed, he realized I had entered the room. "Stage set up?" he asked, sliding the flask into his back pocket.

"Yep," I said, giving him a soft smile. He nodded back at me.

After a silent moment, a bar employee walked by the room and called in, "Band ready?"

"Ready," said Jack, standing up. He gave Wes a short glare before leaving the room. Elena followed right after. Wes took the flask back out for one more swig and walked out too.

"He doesn't care that we brought up his drinking," he began. Then he paused and ran his hand through the top of his hair a couple times. He angled himself toward me more. "He just hates the fact that we noticed he's nervous," explained Munro. I nodded and stared at the couch where they were all just sitting. "I better go. I'll see you after." Munro awkwardly bumped my shoulder with his on the way out. A scent walked with him, something sweet and musky, like oranges and tree bark. I instantly wanted to follow it but I forced myself to wait. *Just a few extra seconds.*

When I let myself walk out of the room and toward the side entrance of the stage, Elena walked up to me.

"Are you gonna stay backstage?" Elena asked.

"Yeah I think so," I said.

"Awesome. Will you hold my cell?" she asked, holding it out for me.

"Of course." I grabbed it from her and she walked to the edge of the stage, fluffed up her curls, and walked on. Claps and a few whoops came from the audience.

"Hi everyone! We're Magnolia's Moon. Tonight we're gonna start with my personal favorite. I'm also dedicating this song to my best friend, Seren, who is backstage right now," Elena started. She looked toward me and waved. Then, turning her gaze back to the audience, she said, "She's always been a big inspiration for me when I write and I think she needs a little inspiration of her own right now." The audience clapped and whooped again. "This one is called 'Yellow.' Hope you enjoy."

Elena swayed in front of the mic as Wes and Jack both started playing a smooth folk melody. Munro kept time with a drumstick on his knee. He looked over, making eye contact with me. He winked slowly in my direction and smiled without his teeth, making the dimples in his cheeks deeper than ever. I grinned back as a warm shiver rushed

down my spine.

Elena started singing:

"She's a girl with a fire in her eyes

And she never seems to say

What's really on her mind.

She's just a girl with her heart out in the light

And her soul comes out at night,

Taking life like it's a fight.

A yellow star, you can see up in the sky.

Sweet as honey, hard as stone,

A little lady who's lost a lot of love.

She's a girl with a fire in her eyes

And she'll never ever say why."

The warm shiver that began with Munro continued

through the entire song, making my cheeks burn for the

band. I couldn't see them, but I could feel their redness.

Normally it would bother me, but I knew I could just blame

it on the hot room this time.

Stars in the Honey

When the set ended after fifteen songs and a couple breaks in between, the audience died down and started mingling amongst themselves. Drunken girls' voices laughed and called inaudible things to the band. I peeked around the corner so I could see the edge of the stage. Three girls stood right under the risen stage, all in short dresses and cowgirl boots. They seemed like the perfect trio of wing-women: one blonde, one brunette, one red-head, all fairly pretty, at least from this distance.

"Oh my god, you were *so* great," the blonde one said. She twirled a strand of her hair between her fingers. Wes walked over and sat down on the end of the stage, hanging his legs off the edge.

At that moment, Elena walked off with the mic stand case. "That girl is trying way too hard," she said, laughing and shaking her head. I laughed too but kept watching.

"I'm Grace," said the brunette. She held her hand out for Wes. He took it and kissed the back softly, staring at her the whole time.

"Wes," he stated, coolly.

The other two, who introduced themselves as Penny (the blonde) and Quinn (the redhead), followed Grace's lead and stuck their hands out too. Wes kissed their hands too.

Jack walked off with his bass case and a speaker. He rolled his eyes at Wes and laughed as he passed me by. I smiled at him and then looked on stage for Munro. He stood behind his drum set, taking bits and pieces off at a time. He already had his glasses back on.

"Who's the drummer?" asked Quinn quietly.

"Ah, that's Munro," Wes said. He turned to look back at Munro. "Dude, come here."

Munro looked up from his drum set and shook his head.

"Come on, this girl wants to say, 'hi,'" Wes tried again.

"Hi," Munro said from his spot. He went back to disassembling.

"Whatever. Sorry," he said to Quinn. She forced a frown and then turned her attention right back to Wes.

Munro packed up one case with things and walked off the stage toward me. He stopped and opened his mouth to talk. He stopped and shook his head slightly.

"What's wrong?" I asked.

He switched the case to his other hand. "He's just already getting on my nerves," he said. He looked back at Wes who, according to the girls' faces, seemed to be telling a *very* interesting story.

"Yeah, I guess he is being kind of a tool," I said. Munro smiled softly. "You guys were great tonight though, your drum solo in 'Luke' was really cool," I added.

"You think so?" he asked. He moved out of the way of a passing employee and faced the light from the stage area. The light distorted his face through his glasses and created little flecks of white in his navy eyes. They looked like tiny stars.

"Yeah. It was really different," I said.

"Thank you," he said. He squinted his eyes into an appreciative smile and walked off.

After everything was packed up into the van, we were all exhausted. Once we got back to the hotel, we left the heavy stuff in the van and went straight up to our rooms. Since it was only around nine thirty, we all changed into pajamas and crowded onto the couch in the living room. Elena picked the movie: *Easy A*. It was one of her favorites and "guilty pleasures" so we had both seen it a million times. The guys weren't quite as interested as we were, but they were happy to just relax for the night.

Jack and Elena sat on the floor, leaning their backs up against the couch. Jack's arm rested around her shoulders. Wes sat in the middle of Munro and I. He crossed his legs in his seat and covered us all in a fluffy blanket. In the scene where Olive gets a singing card, Elena and I sang "Pocket Full of Sunshine" along with the movie at the top of our lungs while the guys just laughed at how ridiculous we probably sounded to our neighbors.

"You two are gonna get us kicked out from noise complaints," said Jack.

"Hey, we are beautiful singers. I'm sure they're enjoying our voices," I said. Elena gave Jack a sassy head nod to agree with me. We quieted down though to actually watch the movie again.

About ten minutes later, Jack was asleep, lightly snoring against Elena's shoulder.

"I'm with Jack here," said Wes, "I'm gonna head to bed." He got up, stepping over Jack and Elena on the ground and walked to our shared room. "Night guys," he added, closing the door behind him.

"Night," Elena and I both replied.

The movie had about half an hour left before Elena and Jack finally gave up too. "Sorry, Seren. I wanna see the 80s movie mashup date proposal but I'm way too tired," she said. She kissed Jack's cheek to wake him up. He stirred and after a couple seconds, opened his eyes.

"Oh dang. Sorry," he said. He ran one hand over his eyes.

"It's okay, baby. Let's go to bed," said Elena. She stood and helped him up. "Wow. I could fall asleep standing up," she added.

"Goodnight. See you in the morning," I said. They walked into their bedroom and shut the door behind them.

Munro and I looked at each other. He wore gray sweatpants and a R.E.M. tank top. His arms were pale but littered with soft tan freckles.

I stretched my legs out onto the couch. "What do you think of the movie?" I asked quietly, trying to focus on the movie instead of Munro.

"It's cute. Not really my kind of movie, but I do like it," he said.

"What're your kind of movies?" I asked.

"Uh mostly thrillers...old horror is cool too. *The Shining. American Psycho.* Things like that," he said. He pulled his legs up onto the couch too, his feet brushing mine as he maneuvered to a comfortable position.

"Really? I love both of those," I said. I turned to face him and he was already looking at me.

"Not your favorites though. What are yours?" he asked back.

"I tend to like older dramas...A Beautiful Mind, No Country for Old Men, The Silence of the Lambs," I started. He smiled and then I added, "My mom really loved Dead Poets Society."

"Oh yeah, that's a great one. You don't like it?" he asked.

I pulled the blankets further up my body. "I just...I haven't watched it in a while."

"Well, we should watch it sometime soon then," he said. One side of his lips turned up into a half smile. He pushed his glasses further up his nose.

I nodded. He turned his attention to the TV again and sank deeper into the couch. I did the same, sinking further into the cushions and under the blanket. I laid my head down on the arm of the chair. I could feel the warmth from his legs just centimeters from my feet, and I desperately wanted to move them closer. I resisted, but thought about it until the credits started rolling.

Chapter 8

When I woke up the next morning, bright yellow light shined through the cracks in the blinds. I rubbed my eyes hard and shifted on my bed. My foot touched something. *Someone.*

I opened my eyes to Elena, Jack, and Wes all standing above me.

"Sleep well?" asked Wes. He sounded annoyed.

I looked around me. *I fell asleep on the couch. With Munro. Oh god.*

"Uh, not really. This couch isn't too comfortable," I mumbled. I looked over at Munro who was somehow still sound asleep. His glasses rested on his nose and he had curled up all the way under the blanket so only his face was visible.

"Wes was gonna make pancakes. Want some?" Elena asked, smiling behind her eyes.

"Yes, please," I stretched out my arms.

Wes rolled his eyes slightly before walking to the kitchen. He grunted while turning on the stove.

"What time is it, anyway?" I asked. Elena sat on the ground next to me. I rolled over to face her.

"It's like nine something," she said. Jack joined Wes in the kitchen. "How was your night after I went to bed?" she whispered.

"It was fine. We just talked about movies for a bit and then I guess we both fell asleep," I said, "I don't remember that though."

"Falling asleep?" she asked.

"Yeah."

"We were all exhausted. I don't blame you," she said. "Nothing else happened though?" she prodded.

"No, I swear."

She made a sour face. "Damn."

"What?" I asked.

"You need a romance, girl," she said, sighing.

"Why is that?" I asked.

"Because, Seren. You haven't dated anyone since that awful skater girl our sophomore year who cheated on you with one of our teachers," Elena said.

"That was just a bad decision on my part overall. I know that," I said, pointing my finger at her. "But I don't *need* a romance. I'm fine."

"Whatever you say. I'm just saying…it'll take your mind off of things…and, you have options," she said. After showing off a huge grin, she stood up and joined the other boys in the kitchen.

After another moment, Munro shifted in his sleep. I gave in this time and ran my foot across his calf, his leg hair tickling me as I moved. He shifted again and half opened his eyes. I settled my foot close to his leg, but not touching. He looked around groggily until his eyes landed on mine.

"Oh, hey," he whispered.

"Hey," I whispered back.

"We fell asleep together?" he asked, kind of questioning it, kind of making a confused statement.

"Mhm," I mumbled. "And Wes doesn't seem too happy about it." I made a "yikes" face and Munro chuckled under his breath. He shifted his position, his leg leaning heavily against my own.

A half hour later we all sat on the floor of the living room in a circle eating Wes' pancakes off of paper plates. A station played the top forty indie songs in the U.S. on the TV in the background. Next to me sat a small jar of peanut butter Elena bought from a convenience store down the block. I slathered my pancakes with it as everyone else talked or started eating.

"What time is our gig today?" asked Wes. He wore a plain white tank top and I could see all of his tattoos straight through it.

"Nine, I think," mumbled Elena through a bite.

"Awesome. We've got all day to explore then," said Wes.

Elena and Jack nodded simultaneously.

"There's a really nice park that I wanna go to," I said before taking a bite of my pancakes.

"I'd like to go too, actually," said Munro. He sat next to me, our knees just an inch apart.

Wes interjected, "Yeah, me too. I'll go."

"How about we all just go? We could all use a little more fresh air on this trip," said Elena. She looked at me and smiled. Her curls were piled on top of her head and she had on a giant sweatshirt and sweats, engulfing her tiny body. We all had two helpings of pancakes and then got dressed for a day outside.

Frank had the morning off since he was really only a driver for the actual gigs and traveling from city to city so Jack decided to drive. We arrived at the general vicinity of the park and found a parking lot for the van near a hiking trail marker.

"This is it?" asked Wes.

"Mhm. The trails are supposed to be really nice," I said, grabbing my backpack and hopping out of the van. Munro followed without a word, grabbing his bag as well. Jack and Elena got out and immediately started walking down the trail, hand in hand. Munro and I followed. Wes eventually lumbered out of the van and down the trail too, staying at least a few feet behind us the entire time.

The trail was all dirt and surrounded by woods of tall green trees and brush. Patches of flowers littered the ground. On the map I had looked at earlier, there were a few ponds here and there around the park that I was excited to see. As we walked, I grabbed my camera from my backpack. I took pictures of anything I found interesting: honeysuckle vines wrapped around trees, black-eyed Susan's surrounding a mossy boulder, a Goldfinch sitting on a branch near the edge of the path.

"You take a lot of pictures," Munro commented as I snapped a picture of the sun shining through the canopy of trees above us.

"It's inspiration," I said, scanning through all of the pictures I'd already taken.

"For what?"

"Screenplays, stories, mise en scène," I said. He gave me a questioning look.

"It's kinda like the arrangement or design of everything on set, like props, scenery, characters..." I said. "Sorry, just technical things."

"No, it's okay. It's interesting," Munro started, "I like films, I just don't know much about them other than genres and my favorite actors and things like that."

"I only know this much because I took the only two film classes DHS offered."

"What were those?" he asked.

"Writing for Film and Media Studies," I answered.

"Those sound interesting. So you like screenwriting the best though? Out of all the film jobs?" he asked.

"Yeah I think so. I didn't do too much on the production side of film but I really like writing so...yeah. I would probably like some of the other creative parts too, like set designer or something."

"That sounds really cool," he said. I snapped a picture of my sneakers in a mud puddle, a light stream got caught in the lens and made it look like some kind of added filter. "Hey, would you maybe want to- "Munro started.

"Guys, look at this!" Wes interjected. He stood in the woods on top of a fallen tree that had gotten caught amongst another tree's lower branches. He climbed further upward.

"Wes, be careful!" yelled Elena. We all stopped to watch.

"I'm fine. You worry too much," he yelled back. Once he was halfway up, about seven feet in the air, the tree's trunk started to bend underneath his weight. There was a sharp sound like bark cracking.

"Wes, come on. Get down," I called. Although I felt at peace between the trees, I hadn't trusted them completely since my mom left. And I definitely didn't trust this one.

"I'm fi- "Wes started, but his foot must have slipped because the next second, he disappeared behind the trunk.

"Wes!?" yelled Elena.

Jack ran off into the woods, jumping over other fallen trees and brush. Munro followed quickly.

"Guys, I'm fine!" we heard from behind the trunk. "Just a scratch," said Wes. He emerged from the brush before Jack and Munro made it to him. A bleeding gash ran across his right bicep.

"Wes, we gotta go to the hospital for that," said Elena as all three guys walked back to the path. When he stepped over the last bit of brush, Elena studied it closer. A leaf stuck to the gooey wound and Elena picked it off gently.

"Uh...yeah, okay. I guess you're right," he agreed. He held his arm close to his body as thick dark blood trickled down to his wrist.

I wore a tank top over my sports bra so I pulled it off and held it out for him.

"Thanks. Can you help?" he asked, starting to reach for it and then realizing he didn't want to let go of his injured arm.

"Of course," I said. I took a couple steps closer to him and wrapped the thin shirt around the gash, making sure to put the pressure in the right spot. I could feel both the sweat and Munro's gaze running down my bare back. I pulled tight on the shirt's knot one more time, and we all started swiftly walking to the van.

On the way to the hospital, I sat with Wes in the middle row and Munro took the backseat. I held a tight grip on Wes' arm to try and stop the blood from seeping more and more through the fabric of my shirt.

"I can hold it," Wes assured.

"No, it's okay. Just relax. I'm sure you don't feel great right now," I said.

He nodded and laid his head back against the top of the seat. Munro took his seatbelt off and leaned forward, resting his arms on the seat in between Wes and I. "Hey, so I was gonna ask before this dip-shit hurt himself…" Munro started.

Wes raised his head and looked back. "Hey. I was just being adventurous," he stated.

"More like stupid," called Elena from the front seat.

"Anyway…" Munro continued, "would you maybe wanna go out for an early dinner tomorrow before our last show in Nashville?"

Wes groaned and laid his head back down.

"Oh…" I thought about it. *What if it doesn't go well and we're awkward the rest of the trip?*

Wes watched my face intently as I thought the idea through.

Munro continued, "If you don't want to, it's totally okay. I just thought…you know, I'd like to hear more about your screenwriting and the set designing and I thought that would be a good time for that." He studied my face, his dark eyes scanned mine behind his glasses.

I looked at him and then at Wes, who sat in an annoyed stupor. I shook my head at Wes and at the fact that I knew there was a huge chance this could hurt more than help me right now, but I was going to say yes anyway.

"Yeah. Let's do it," I said.

He smiled, bright teeth showing. His dimples sunk deep into his pink cheeks like the black holes in space movies. He didn't smile like that often.

"Guys, can we like, hurry up, maybe?" moaned Wes, raising his head back up again. He looked at me. His eyes seemed to glaze over.

"Yeah, how close is the hospital?" I asked, looking around at our surroundings. We still seemed to be in park territory by the way the trees crowded against the edge of the road.

"It's pretty close. Like ten more minutes," said Jack. Elena held the map on her phone back for me to see. I nodded at her and turned my attention back to Wes.

"Just focus on something else and we'll be there soon," I assured him. He nodded and stared at my face the rest of the ride.

Chapter 9

We arrived back at the hotel three hours later. It took an hour to get to the hospital and get into an actual room. Jack was the only one allowed in, but he recounted the other two hours to us. The doctors took forever to see Wes and decided that he needed stitches in his arm. The five stitches only took about ten minutes to do but getting him checked out took just as long as getting him checked in. The doctors also gave him pain meds and something to ward off infection since he must have cut it on tree bark or a limb, something not very sanitary.

The minute we walked into our hotel room, Wes made a straight shot to his bed and laid down. We only had a couple more hours until we needed to leave for their second Nashville gig.

"I'm gonna start getting ready. Makeup is calming and I *need* some relaxation right now," said Elena. She walked into her and Jack's room to grab her makeup bag. "You wanna join me in here?" she called out to me.

"Yeah! Let me grab my stuff," I called back.

Jack and Munro sat on the couch and turned the TV onto some sports channel. Soccer players ran across the screen.

I walked into Wes and I's room. He laid face first into the bed. His wounded arm, wrapped up in gauze, fell off the side of the bed.

"Wes, you gotta keep that elevated," I said softly. I didn't know if he had already fallen asleep or not. He groaned. *Not quite asleep.*

I walked to him and turned his body over onto his back. I bent over and wrapped my arms around his chest and scooted his body upward so his head, shoulder, and back were slightly propped up by his pillows. Then, I grabbed a pillow from my own bed and slid it up under his right arm.

"Do you need anything?" I asked.

Silence.

It was like taking care of my mom again, before she left. She wouldn't sit up at all for those bad months, and when I was actually home, I would have to go into her room and prop her up so she could try to eat or so she wouldn't get terrible back aches that made her silently cry.

I sat in there with her a couple times. We wouldn't talk - just sit. Once I brought one of her favorites books in: "The Light Between Oceans" by M. L. Stedman. I got through one chapter that day and promised to read to her again the next time. But that was the only chapter I ever got to read.

It still sits on her bedside table to this day, a bookmark settled in the crook next to, "Chapter 2."

I took a deep breath. After making sure Wes' arm was lifted enough and wouldn't slide off the pillow, I grabbed my makeup bag from my suitcase and took it to Elena's bathroom across the hotel room. She sat on one of the counters tracing winged eyeliner on the top of her right eye.

"Hey girl," she said, focusing on her face in the mirror.

"Hey. Are you sure Wes is gonna be fine to play tonight? He seems pretty out of it," I said, setting my bag on the counter and hopping up to join her. She finished her one eye and turned to do the other.

"He'll be fine. One time in high school, he fractured a bone in his ankle at the beginning of a soccer game, took four Advil, and kept playing until the end when he could barely even form the words to say, 'I think I broke my leg.' Even made three goals that day." She paused, looked at me, and shrugged. "At least that's what Jack told me."

"I guess we'll see," I said. I pulled out my primer and foundation.

Elena finished her other eye and turned her body toward me, leaning up against the wall at the end of the counter. She placed her feet on the opposite side of one of the sinks.

"So, you have a date with Munro tomorrow?" she asked, a sly smirk hiding behind her eyes as she watched for my reaction.

"Yeah, apparently," I said. I tried to keep my face emotionless.

"Should be fun. He's liked you for a while," she said. She picked up an eyeshadow pallet and started blending a dark maroon into the outer corners of her eyes.

"Wait, what? I thought Wes liked me for a while," I replied.

"Well, I mean, Wes has thought you were hot since day one... Well, okay maybe not day one. We were both still in that weird goth phase freshmen year, you know?

But like the first time we all kinda hung out as a group -
you, me, Jack, and Wes. I think it was for Jack's birthday
maybe? Our sophomore year. Right after he and I started
dating," she explained. She swiped too far with her brush
and a maroon streak formed on her cheek. "Shit."

"Okay, but Munro?" I prodded.

"Right," she began, taking a cotton pad and
rubbing off the streak. "So that first rehearsal you came to
at Jack's apartment…"

"Mhm." I squirted primer onto my fingers and
started rubbing it into my face. It mixed in with leftover
sweat and I instantly regretted not washing my face first.

"When you left to drive home, Munro stayed after
for like an hour just going on and on to Jack about how
cool he thought you were. You and him apparently had a
tipsy conversation about your favorite summer music or
something. Granted, he was still pretty drunk. He had to
crash at Jack's before going home…but he still seemed to

really like you," Elena continued. She blended more dark colors into her eyelids.

"Why hasn't he tried anything until now?" I asked.

"He's quiet. And he gets pretty nervous talking to people in general…but especially any time before or right after a gig. I'm surprised he scouted you out after the gig yesterday."

"You saw that?"

"Yeah, I was coming back out to grab something off the stage but you two were blocking the hall so I waited. I think you two would be cute together," she said. She finished blending her eyeshadow and set her palette down. "I still don't get how you do your foundation first."

I dumped a little glob of the palest foundation I could find at the drugstore from the frosted glass bottle onto my hand. "I don't get how you do your eyes first."

"It's just easier! No fall-out!" she laughed.

"Well, maybe you should just be better at eyeshadow," I said back. She nudged me with her foot and made a face. Then she smiled and grabbed her phone. She put on her "Getting Ready" playlist and Avril Lavigne's song "Hot" started to play. We sang along to every word at the top of our lungs, partially so Elena could warm up and partially because it was a getting ready tradition for us.

When we parked outside the gig venue, blinding lights entered the van's windows. I looked out and saw the marquee sign lit up with "Playing Tonight: Ben and the Breakers and Magnolia's Moon" in big block letters. We drove around to the alley again and parked next to a graffitied door that read, "Stage Entrance."

Wes hopped out of the car with his usual pep. The band decided to do maroon accents in their outfits today instead of all black. Wes wore faded maroon cut-off shorts, all black Converse, and a way-too-long tank that showed off his arm tattoos and a little sliver of his abs on either side. I followed him around to the trunk in jean shorts and a silky black tank. My hair was tied back off my forehead with a silver headscarf. The rest of the band jumped out of the car to help too. Elena had on a long black dress with a maroon rose in her hair, stuck behind one ear. Jack wore a maroon button-down with black khaki pants that barely reached his ankles and black loafers with maroon printed socks. Munro climbed out of the backseat last, sporting a black and maroon tie-dye t-shirt, black shorts, and black vans. His silver rings cluttered his fingers.

Wes grabbed his guitar case with his good arm and then looked down at the bandages on his other. "Uh, Seren, could you carry in my guitar amp for me?" he asked.

I nodded my head. "Of course." I picked it up with both arms and followed him to the backstage area of the bar. The others came in one by one after us.

This bar was bigger than the first, with a huge lounge area littered with different colored couches and a few coffee tables made from trunks. The walls of the room were covered in past gig posters. While sitting on any of the couches, you could see onto the stage through a wide slit in black velvet curtains. The other band played a pop-rock vibe song on the stage that we could clearly hear from the back room. Magnolia's Moon was on after their next song.

Wes sat down with his guitar on a yellow suede couch and started taking it out. He set the base of the guitar on his lap and held up the neck with his left hand. I sat next to him, on his right side and watched, waiting if he needed any help. Munro sat on the other side of me but focused on the music magazines littered over every surface in the room.

"I think…If I can rest my right arm on something while I play, I'll be fine," Wes said quietly.

"Maybe we can pull a chair out for you? And maybe one of those little side-table things?" I asked.

"Yeah, yeah. That could work," he said.

I got up and pulled a wooden chair over and then grabbed a little metal side-table to set next to it.

"Try it out," I said.

I walked over and made sure he got up off the sinking couch okay. He handed the guitar to me and I grabbed it as he used his left arm to push himself to standing. He sat down in the chair and rested his right arm on the side-table.

"I think this one might be too tall," he said. I looked around for another and found a short stool that reached just below Wes' hips when he sat.

"How about this one?" I asked, bringing it over.

"Let's try," he said. I handed him the guitar and switched out the tables. "Yeah, that should work," he said, smiling. His right elbow rested on the stool in just the right spot so his right hand could strum. His bandaged bicep bulged like a Greek god.

"It doesn't hurt like that?" I asked. The music from the stage had stopped so I strained to look. The other band yelled a thank you and started packing up their things.

When I looked back, Wes was already looking up at me. He played a chord and winced just slightly. "Not bad at all," he said, grinning.

I nodded. He started playing, getting into the rhythm of fingering the strings with a damaged arm. After a bit, I realized I had been staring at the bandage for a little too long.

My thoughts were interrupted as Patrick came in and asked, "Ready guys? We're all set up out there." A multitude of "yeah"s and "mhm"s bounced around the room.

"Can you bring these out there too?" I asked Patrick, lifting up the stool and gesturing toward the chair Wes still sat in.

"Oh, yep," said Patrick. He walked to Wes and helped him up before carrying the chair off to the stage. Wes carried his guitar with one hand and started following Patrick.

"Wait. I have an idea," I said. Wes paused and turned toward me. I untied the handkerchief from my hair and wrapped it neatly around Wes' bandages. I tied it in a messy knot and nodded my head. "What do you think? A new fashion statement?" I asked. I looked up at him.

He smiled widely and nodded. "It looks great. Thanks, Seren." He leaned over and left a sloppy peck on my temple before walking off to the stage.

I started to follow too, with the stool, but before I got far, Jack stopped me. "I'll take it," he said. "That was cool of you."

"Oh, thanks," I said. Jack walked off to the stage.

Elena walked from behind me and hugged me around the neck. "See? I told you you'd be great at this job."

"One, this still isn't my job. And two, I didn't keep him out of trouble. I just helped him keep his cool guy image," I explained.

"Whatever you say," she said, walking around in front of me, "You're still doing great."

As she walked away, I smiled to myself. *I am pretty good at the whole taking-care-of-people-thing.*

Then Munro walked up. "What was all that?" he asked, nodding toward Wes on stage. He was sitting down in his chair, getting the guitar situated to a comfortable spot.

"What?" I asked.

"That kiss," Munro answered, not fully looking me in the eye. There was no anger in his face, just a longing distance.

"He was just thanking me for helping him out with the staging stuff," I explained.

"Right," he said flatly. He lingered nearby for a few more seconds before nodding and walking toward the stage.

Before he sat down behind his drum set, he pulled his drum sticks out of the back pocket of his shorts. Elena looked back at him, making eye contact, and he nodded

back. She turned toward the audience, introduced their

band, and cued the guys to start playing.

Chapter 10

My mom's singing crept into my dreams at around six A.M. before the sun started shining through the cracks in the curtains. I woke up and tears formed at the edges of my eyes but I held them in. I hummed the melody of "Syrup and Honey" as softly as I could until I fell back asleep again.

An hour later at seven A.M. I woke up again from another dream, or I guess, a nightmare. I found my dad out in his garden, lying facedown on his table, not moving, not breathing. In his notebook, there was just one word written in scraggly small letters: "Seren." I woke up the moment I looked straight into his still-open eyes. I fell back asleep again after grabbing a glass of water from the kitchenette.

Finally, at eight A.M. I decided to stop all of it. I got out of bed and changed into cropped leggings and a sports bra. I grabbed a towel from the bathroom and sneaked out onto the balcony.

I stood on the balcony, looking past the cast-iron fencing and out toward the city. The sun had only been up for about an hour and everyone seemed to be up and moving already. Cars raced down all of the streets, sunlight bouncing off one windshield onto another. Pedestrians walked quickly down the sidewalks, avoiding each other and eye contact. A couple blocks down the street, an old man sat in a lawn chair on the roof of a shorter building. He read the newspaper in just his underwear, slippers, and sunglasses.

I laid the towel down on the concrete floor and sat down, cross-legged on it. The rough fabric grazed against my skin but I shook off the feeling. I rested my hands lightly on top of my knees and closed my eyes. The air was muggy. I could feel droplets of humidity forming on my top layer of skin.

I took a deep breath in. Rust and asphalt. *Not like home, but it's okay.*

I followed my natural breathing pace and focused on making each breath last the same length of time. I rolled my neck back and forth, trying to ease the slight kink in my neck from sleeping wrong. The stretch felt good so I continued. I stretched and meditated until finally, I turned and sat facing the city again. I watched the honey-yellow sun slowly rise further and further into the sky.

Later that day, Elena and I had gone on a girl's day shopping trip and ended up in a thrift store a few blocks from our hotel. The walls were covered in colorful tapestries and scarves hung all across the ceilings. We scoured the racks of vintage, oddly patterned clothing. After an hour and a half, we'd gone through every aisle and every item of clothing and carried a full arms load each.

"Do you girls need help with fitting rooms?" asked an employee with the longest, bleach blonde dreads I'd ever seen. She smiled, and I noticed two tiny holes below her lower lip where she had once had a spider bite piercing.

Elena and I both laughed as we answered, "yes," straining over the piles of clothes in our arms to actually make any eye contact with her.

"Give me just a minute," the employee said. She walked over to a box sitting on the ground and took out two identical cloth bags. She walked back to us and opened one up in front of me. "Toss some in there, and you can take this back to the rooms with you."

"Thank you," I said, dumping half of my pile into the bag. Elena did the same and the employee carried the bags back for us as we carried the rest of the clothes we still had in our arms.

"My name is Roxie. Yell if you need anything else," she said, leaving us in a small back room decorated with hot pink walls and dim light fixtures. Three little cubbies sat against the back wall and a different tapestry hung in front of each to act as a privacy curtain.

"This is gonna take a while," Elena said, taking the half pile in her arms and hanging them up inside one of the cubbies.

"It's okay. We've got like two hours left...that'll be enough right?" I asked.

Elena made a "I really hope so" face and we both went into our cubbies to start trying things on.

"Maybe you can find something cute for your date later," said Elena from the next cubby over.

Fuck. I totally forgot.

"That's true... I think I grabbed a few dresses. I'll just have to find them," I said. Just then, I heard Roxie's voice talking to someone outside. I peeked my head out, having already taken off my shirt.

"Hey, Roxie?" I called out.

"Yep?" she answered, coming around a corner into the back room.

"I'm sorry to ask this but could you possibly go through that bag and pick out all of the dresses? We're kinda in a hurry and I totally forgot about this date thing I'm going on…" I explained.

"No problem. Start trying other things on and I'll throw any dresses I find on the hook," she said, pointing to a red-painted metal hook screwing into the outside of my cubby.

"Perfect. Thank you so much," I said, ducking back inside.

I stripped off my shorts and found a dress in the pile of clothes I had already brought inside. I pulled it over my head and looked in the mirror. On the hanger, the dress looked like a cool vintage find, but on my body, it hung loosely down to my kneecaps and blended into my own pale skin tone. I pulled my tapestry back and asked Elena to come out and see.

"This is bad, right?" I asked. Roxie and Elena both stared at the dress.

"Yeah, not good," said Elena.

Roxie shook her head. "I like the sequins but you kinda look naked under them. Not the right nude for you," she commented. "I found a couple dresses. Try one of those on," she added, starting to scour through the rest of the bag. Elena went back into her cubby. I turned, grabbing the dresses from the hook, and headed back into mine as well.

"This one is nice," I said. The simple navy dress hit mid-thigh which always looked good on anyone. I stepped out again.

Elena poked her head out from behind her tapestry. "Oh, yes. I like that one a lot. Goes well with your hair too," she said.

I kept the tapestry open but stepped back inside my cubby to look in the mirror again. The neckline hit right below my clavicle and wrapped around to my back elegantly. The fabric was reliable enough to not be see-through and to hold its shape all night too.

"That's it," Roxie said, coming back around the corner from the between the racks of clothes in the store. "Got shoes to go with it?" she asked.

I shook my head.

"Stay there," she instructed.

I leaned against the doorway of my cubby and Elena stepped out in a metallic silver tube top and matching bowl-shaped skirt. "I like her," she said, matter-of-factly. I laughed and nodded to agree.

Munro and I left the hotel and walked down the street to a tiny, secluded Italian restaurant a few streets over. We fit right in with our accidentally-matching outfits. He wore a navy suit with no tie and a plain white button-up, along with dark gray, suede oxfords, and his clear-framed glasses. His hair was styled back, slicked so smooth that it didn't look real. I somehow also wore gray shoes. At the store, Roxie had picked out plain gray pumps from their shoe wall, and although I was skeptical on not wearing black or ripped or bleached anything, I ended up feeling really good in the outfit Roxie basically decided on for me.

We stepped into the restaurant and a waiter dressed in black slacks and a white button-down immediately asked us, "Just you two?"

"Yes," Munro answered.

"Follow me," said the waiter. He sat us at a small circular table in the center of the room. It was covered in a dark red tablecloth, two wine glasses, two water glasses, two sets of silverware, and had a tea light candle as the centerpiece.

The waiter handed us menus and said, "My name is Alex. Can I start you off with any drinks tonight?"

"I'll take your house red, please," said Munro.

"Alright. ID?" asked Alex. Munro took his wallet out and showed it to Alex. "Perfect. And what about you?" he asked in my direction.

"Just a water would be great," I replied.

"Lovely. I will be back with those in a moment," said Alex. He set two menus onto the table before turning away.

Munro raised an eyebrow at me. "I thought you had a fake?" he whispered, leaning in to the table.

"I do…I just didn't bring it tonight," I explained.

"Oh, I'm sorry," he said, cheeks turning a little pinker. "I wouldn't have gotten anything…"

"No, no, it's okay," I interrupted. "You can have all the wine you want."

He chuckled lightly. "If you're okay with it," he said.

I nodded and smiled back.

"So," Munro started, leaning back in his chair again. He grabbed a menu and scanned it. "I'm thinking spaghetti. I read online when I looked it up that this place serves everything in huge portions so we could share if you wanted," he said.

"Is the sauce meatless?" I asked, grabbing the other menu off the table and opening it to check.

"I hope so. I'm vegetarian," he said, eyes still on the menu.

"Oh right, I knew that. No bacon," I said.

He looked up and smirked slightly, dimples deepening. "No bacon."

We paused and watched each other's expressions. His smirk softened, lips turning up on both sides into a light smile.

He shook his head slightly, like he was waking himself up from a dream. "So, spaghetti is okay though? With no meat?" he asked.

"Yep," I said, folding my menu back together and setting it on the table.

Alex came back at the perfect moment, pouring Munro his wine and me a glass of water. He picked my wine glass off the table to take away. "Have you decided on an entree?" he asked.

"Can we get the spaghetti with no meat?" asked Munro.

"Of course, sir." Alex said. He nodded, grabbed the menus from the table, and walked off.

We stayed silent for a moment. I noticed a pianist sitting at a baby grand off in one corner. He trifled through pages on the music stand, deciding on a piece to play.

"So," Munro started again, "I've heard a little about your dad and you've told me one of your mom's favorite movies but I don't know much else about your family. Do you have any brothers or sisters?" he asked.

I instantly remembered why I hadn't gone out on any dates in a while. They always started with a family question.

"I just live with my dad. My grandma lives kind of close too but that's really all the family I have," I said, hoping he'd go off on a better subject.

"Your mom doesn't live with you?" he asked.

There it is.

"Um…" I started. I hated this part, telling people my mom died. No, telling people that my mom killed herself. That was always the worst. The look on people's faces when I say that my own mother decided to leave the world, leave her daughter, instead of finding help or just "getting over" the fact that her son died before he was even born.

"Uh," I started again, "Well, my mom committed suicide when I was eleven."

Munro's face turned a grayish white.

"Oh," he said.

"It's been a long time. It's fine," I said, taking a gulp of water from my glass.

"That must have been really hard," he said.

I've heard that one before. "Yeah," I replied.

I shouldn't be so hard on him. People never know what to say…he isn't any different.

"I'm sure you have a lot of good memories with her though, right? I mean, favorite movies, favorite songs, traditions and things…" he said. He gave me a comforting smile. "If you don't mind, I'd love to hear about her."

My breath caught in my lungs. They always want to know how I took it, why she left, what was wrong, or just ignore the topic completely after I tell them.

I wasn't sure how much I could say without tears starting to run down my face but I began anyway, "Her name was Elodie. That's my middle name."

Munro leaned into the table again, resting his elbows on it and resting his chin on top of his folded hands. "I've never heard that name before."

"It's not very common. It's French. My great-great-grandma was from France," I continued, "Anyway, uh, yeah. Her name was Elodie. She, uh, went to the same high school as me and graduated from a college in Chicago and had me pretty soon after. She never really got a job after that, but most weekends she worked at the Danville library, which is where I started working a few summers ago."

"Did it make you feel any closer to her?" he asked.

"A little. When I was younger, I'd go with her sometimes and read children's books on the floor while she worked. I was always a quiet kid, so she knew I wouldn't cause any problems. I'd just sit there all day long. Every once in a while, I'd catch her peeking through the book racks to check on me. This is kind of ridiculous… but when I started working there, sometimes I'd feel her looking through the racks at me again. Obviously, she was never there though. It was a weird feeling."

"That's really cool. Who knows? Maybe she was actually watching you somehow," Munro said.

I watched his face light up as the thought occurred to him. For some reason, at that moment, I wanted to crawl up next to him on a couch and spill everything about my mom and my weird, sad life to him all at once. He would listen and not say anything stupid like some people did: "Why didn't you try and stop it?" *I did. Everyone did.* "Why didn't she take her meds?" *How were we supposed to get her to take her meds if we couldn't even get her to*

eat or sit up in bed?

I wanted to rant to him about every stupid thing anyone had ever said about my mom, everything anyone had ever said to me. But, I kept it to myself. I needed to wait. An Italian restaurant with a soft jazz pianist playing in the background was not the right place.

"What about traditions? Anything you two always did?" he asked.

"Well…the peanut butter pancakes thing was from her. She loved peanut butter. Sometimes she'd add honey on top too," I said.

"What else?" he asked, his eyes focused on mine, begging to read every thought inside my head.

"Every day on her birthday, we'd go outside in the backyard and have a picnic lunch. Sometimes we'd have pancakes for lunch, sometimes we'd eat her other favorites like pumpkin bread and fresh watermelon and…" I trailed off. My mind went blank.

"Munro…" I started again, "What day is it?"

"Uh, hold on," he said. He grabbed his phone from his pocket and clicked it on. "It's June twelfth. Why?"

My hands started shaking. A couple drops of water fell from my glass as I tried setting it back down on the table. All of the air inside my lungs dissipated and I couldn't breathe anymore.

"Today," I wheezed out. I tried standing up and my legs felt wobbly, especially in the heels, but I forced myself. "It's her birthday. Today," I said.

I didn't wait for Munro. I grabbed my purse from behind my chair and ran out of the restaurant. Outside, I jogged as far as I could in my new heels, taking breaths only when I absolutely needed them. The air was hot and stuck to the inside of my mouth. I wanted to choke.

I ran down the street and into a side alley littered with trash bags and debris. I leaned back against one of the brick walls and gasped. The thick air wouldn't let me take a full breath. My lungs wouldn't fill. I collapsed to the ground, feeling the rough brick scrape against my bare shoulders. I closed my eyes and took the pain.

I forgot her.

"Seren?" I heard Munro yell from the street. I heard his footsteps start to jog by the alley, and then he stopped. I didn't open my eyes.

"Seren? Seren, are you okay?" he asked. He bent down next to me and I could feel his warm breath on my neck.

"Oh my god," I groaned. I opened my eyes and the alley started spinning. "Go away," I forced out.

"What?" Munro asked.

I looked straight into his eyes and the blue darkness calmed me down just enough to gain strength back in my legs. I stood up. "Please, go away," I said a little clearer. I bent down, holding in the urge to vomit from vertigo, and pulled off my heels one at a time.

"I'm not leaving you here, Seren," Munro said.

"Fine," I said. I took a couple steps and then turned back toward him. "You can stay here then, and I'll go." I turned back around but he pulled me back around by my wrist.

"Where are you going? We can find somewhere to sit and we can just talk about it. It's okay," he assured.

"It is *not* okay. I forgot my own mother's fucking birthday. I have had a picnic in my backyard every single birthday since she's left me and this year, I just forgot. I forgot about my mom. And I can't fix it," I said, my voice raising louder than I'd ever heard it before.

Munro stood near the brick wall, a little slumped over, wide-eyed.

"I forgot my mom," I said again. I turned and walked away.

He didn't try to follow me.

Chapter 11

I got back to the hotel. The band must have all gone out for dinner because the room was completely empty. I went straight to Wes and I's room and laid down in bed, covering myself up in the sheets and comforter. My body felt so exhausted that after just a couple seconds, I was fast asleep.

"Seren, you gotta get ready. We've got half an hour before we gotta leave." Elena's voice slithered under the covers and into my ear.

I lifted the covers off myself and turned to look at her. She stood above my bed, all done up and in the black dress from the thrift store.

"Oh, you're still in your dress," she commented.

I made some sort of groan.

"I know you're still groggy from napping but you gotta get up if you're coming to the gig. We could really use some extra help tonight," she continued.

"Okay, okay," I mumbled out.

"Cool," she said and then skipped out of the room.

I slid out from under the covers and dragged my suitcase into the bathroom. I could hear Wes, Munro, and Jack having a conversation in the living room. I slammed the bathroom door behind me and ran the water from the sink.

I stared into the mirror. I looked stoned. The whites of my eyes were pink, and it was a struggle for me to open them all the way. My lips were dry, little lines forming in the dark pink cushion. I bent down and splashed handfuls of water onto my face. It didn't help my appearance much but it felt nice.

I wiped off some running mascara from under my eyes and added more to my top lashes. Then I added a little concealer under my eyes to hide some of the purple emerging from under my skin. After that, I shrugged at myself in the mirror. *As good as it's going to get*, I thought.

I unzipped the dress and let it fall off my body. I turned around, looking at my shoulders in the mirror now. They were a dark pink color and red lines ran criss-crossed through the patches. I shuffled around in my suitcase and came back up with a band tee that covered my shoulders fully. Then I added forest green, corduroy shorts and my Dr. Martens to the ensemble. I gave myself one last look over in the mirror and walked out to join the group.

The van stayed completely silent on the way to the bar besides the latin music playing in the background that Frank chose before we left. I sat in the back row by myself, sprawled out across the seats, scrolling through every social media app I had on my phone to pass the time and avoid eye contact with anyone else in the van.

At the venue, Munro avoided me at all costs. He stood near the stage waiting, swaying back and forth nervously. Did he want to stay away or did he just think that I wanted him to stay away?

Wes paced back and forth in the band's waiting room. It looked incredibly like the bar's waiting room from the night before except they had actual coffee tables, and all of their couches and chairs were a dark green that matched my shorts almost perfectly.

"Why is he so nervous?" I whispered to Elena who sat next to me, fixing up her purple nail polish.

"A writer from Under the Radar is here," she said.

"What's Under the Radar?" I asked.

Jack interjected, "One of the coolest indie music magazines. He's read every issue he can find. If we get a good review, even just an online one that never goes to print, it would really help us get the kind of gigs that we need."

I nodded my head in an understanding manner. After another ten minutes, they all took the stage. It couldn't have gone any better and afterward, the band decided to go out for drinks to celebrate.

I asked Frank to drive me home claiming to feel sick so Elena wouldn't ask too many questions.

The next morning, we all woke up at eight A.M. to start our drive to Louisville for the next four nights. There wasn't much talking again. Every once in a while, a song that Elena and I knew would come on the radio and we'd sing along. Jack and Elena made short comments to each other every few minutes in the middle row. About an hour in, Jack and Wes, who sat on the other side of the back row with me, had an argument about how many pet dogs they'd had their entire lives. I don't remember Munro saying one word.

After the three hour drive, we arrived at an apartment complex. Frank parked the van in a spot on the side of the road and we all got out, staring up at the six-story, black brick, building.

"Are you sure this is it?" Elena called to Frank as he started to unpack the van.

"Yep!" he answered.

"Okay, let's grab our stuff," said Jack with a shrug. He walked around the back of the van and rolled suitcase after suitcase onto the sidewalk. I threw my bag over my shoulder and started rolling my suitcase inside.

The lobby was quaint with white tile floors, dark gray walls, a door to the mailboxes on one wall, a door for the employees in the back, stairs, and one elevator. A little desk with an apartment secretary guard sat in the middle of the lobby toward the back wall. Frank shoved his way ahead of us all and checked us in at the desk. He grabbed our keys and sent us up. He and Patrick were staying nearby in a hotel.

"I guess my parents decided an Airbnb was better than a hotel room this time," Munro said, pressing the up button next to the elevator.

We took the elevator up all six floors to the top and walked down a long hallway to the very end.

"This is it," said Munro. He unlocked the door and led us all inside.

The door opened up into a living room, adorned with white leather couches and armchairs, a glass coffee table, and a flat-screen TV set into a wide glass entertainment system. To the back of the living room was an open doorway that led to a small kitchen. There were four other doorways and we all set our stuff down instantly to explore. Three of the doors were bedrooms: one queen sized bed, one full, and one set of bunk-beds. The other door led to a huge bathroom with a toilet, double sinks, a glass shower, and a claw-foot ceramic tub.

"Alright," Elena started once we all converged in the living room again, "I think it'd be best if Jack and I took the queen, Seren took the full, and Wes and Munro took the bunks."

Everyone nodded silently in agreement.

"Okay. All set. Let's get moved in," she said.

Chapter 12

An hour went by before all of us gathered back into the living room.

"I'm hungry," complained Wes.

"I am too. All I had on the drive was donut holes," said Jack.

"Do you guys have a gig tonight?" I asked.

"Nope. Our first one here is tomorrow evening," said Elena.

"Let's go out tonight!" said Wes, growing excited.

"I'm down," said Elena. Jack and Munro both nodded. "Seren?" she asked, staring in my direction.

"Oh, uh…I don't know," I said. I ran my fingers through my tangled hair a few times.

"Come on, it'll be fun. This will be our first time out this year without any of us having to perform first," Elena pushed, laughing light-heartedly.

I let out a sigh. "Okay, sure. Where should we go?" I asked, giving in. A twinge of excitement arose in my chest as I thought about going out with Elena like we used to.

We both got fake IDs at sixteen and started going out to dance clubs every weekend. We would grab a drink or two, usually a long island iced tea for me and a tequila sunrise for Elena, and just sway in the middle of the crowd, forgetting about school and relationships and family.

"Somewhere with food first," said Wes.

"We'll pick a club first and I'm sure there will be a restaurant or something nearby," Elena said.

The club stood next to a hole-in-the-wall grocery store and a LGBTQ-geared bookstore. The outside brick was painted black like our apartment building and one circular sign the size of a basketball hung above the doorway. It read, "Aura" in neon blue letters.

After stuffing our faces full of street gyros down the block at a walk-up cafe, we made our way to the end of the short line outside the club. Elena and I matched in chunky black heels and dresses, hers, a dark purple with a deep plunge neck, and mine, black with velvet leopard spots and an open back. She added dangly silver earrings to her outfit while I chose my same silver headscarf that I had put on Wes' arm earlier in the week. The guys all wore different colored button-down shirts, shorts, and nice sneakers. Wes tied a yellow bandana that matched his shirt around his head to keep his hair out of his eyes. Munro decided on contacts instead of his glasses and a dark green shirt. Jack added a purple tie to match Elena.

Elena, Jack, and I all used our fakes to get in and once inside, our entire group stuck together to get to the bar and order drinks. The left side of the building was a wall-to-wall bar lined with tall black metal chairs. The middle was a dance floor with black and white checkered tile and multicolored lights moving back and forth in every direction. Toward the back was the DJ stand where two guys in all-white oversized clothes remixed the popular pop and electronic songs together and took requests from overly-drunk girls in bra-tops. Across the room from the bar, past the dance floor, were the bathrooms where long lines of people already stood, even though it was only around ten o'clock.

"Long Island, please!" I yelled to a bartender.

Elena caught one too and yelled for two Whiskey Sours. Wes and Munro stood behind and waited somewhat patiently for their own turn to order.

"Let's go dance!" yelled Elena over the music once we were both handed our drinks. I nodded to her and followed her to the dance floor. Elena held her free hand out behind her and I grabbed it with mine as we weaved through the dancing crowd. We found a comfortable spot smack in the middle and started to sip and dance.

Elena's dancing always started at the top of her body: she moved her shoulders around in circular movements and her head swayed back and forth to the beat. Her eyes closed when she felt the music dig deep into her body and opened again when that feeling left her.

My dancing, on the other hand, started and mostly stayed at and below my hips. I moved around on my feet, shuffling them back and forth and swaying my hips side to side and around in circles. We were both so different in our dancing but we had both been told at one time or another that we were good dancers. We never cared if we were good, we just liked dancing together.

Elena moved closer and wrapped her free arm around my neck. She kept swaying in between drinks. Both guys and girls snuck glances at us both between the other moving bodies around us.

I took a long sip of my drink and winced a bit.

"How is it!?" Elena yelled over the music, just a couple inches from ear.

"Good!" I yelled back. "And strong!" I added, letting out a laugh. She nodded.

There was a short break in the intense dance music and Elena and I took a breather, both looking around the room at our surroundings. Wes broke through the crowd from the direction of the bar. He pulled his bandana down toward his eyes and then back up, wiping up the sweat on his forehead. His cheeks were flushed and wet. The moving lights bounced off them and made him glitter as he walked toward us.

He waved through the crowd to us with his free hand, making sure not to spill his drink in the other.

"Where are Jack and Munro?" asked Elena once he got close enough to hear.

"Munro wasn't ready to be on the dance floor so Jack stayed back at the bar with him," Wes said.

The music started to get loud and more upbeat again so she had to strain to be heard. "I'm almost done

with my drink so I'm gonna head back to the bar now too!"
she yelled into my ear again.

I nodded reluctantly and she squeezed my arm
before walking away.

Wes and I stood for a moment, neither of us really
knowing what to do next. I almost followed Elena to the
bar. *Maybe I should talk to Munro? Maybe I overreacted?*

I glanced over at the bar, through the crowd of
dancing people, and caught a glimpse of him. He leaned
against the bar. A tall girl in tight leather shorts and a black
bralette leaned generously close to his back and kept trying
to make eye contact but he didn't seem to notice. He
simply stared into whatever drink he had in his hand and
nodded at the words Jack and Elena seemed to be spewing
at him over the music.

My feet made a couple steps toward the bar and
then an amped-up version of "Untouched" by The
Veronicas came on and I *had* to dance.

Wes watched me as I started swaying again. I

avoided eye contact at first, staring at anything but his face: the murky floor, his t-shirt sleeve that barely covered the bandage on his bicep, the one wave that curled up around his earlobe. Then his good hand reached out and wrapped itself around my waist.

I looked up and he was staring at me, a wide grin spreading across his tanned face. I noticed the little patches of red hair in his growing scruff. They framed his lips, thin but bright pink in the club light like the meat of a grapefruit.

I didn't think about it for a second. There was just some invisible force that pulled my body toward his. I think it just felt nice to let go for once. At that moment, I just wanted to let myself feel some form of happiness, some form of excitement.

Wes' hand reached the small of my back and he pulled me in even tighter. My chest pressed against his. I could feel the ridges of his abs through his shirt. I laid my free hand on his chest and ran my finger along his collarbone as we swayed into each other, hips against hips, thigh between thighs.

I looked up at him. He smiled and I returned it.

Past Wes' shoulder, Munro stood near the edge of the dance floor. He watched as Wes and I's bodies moved together as one. He had watched me lean myself into Wes, feeling his pelvis grind softly into my own, Wes' hand gripping my back hard to keep us from separating. We made eye contact. He lingered a moment longer and then walked off.

Wes noticed too. "Don't worry about him," he said loudly into my ear. From how loud the music was, it was the equivalent of a whisper in a normal volume room.

I watched his face as he assured me everything would be fine and I nodded. We danced for another song.

When the beat died down again, Wes leaned his face in. His lips grazed mine and I let it happen. My body went almost limp in his grip and our lips felt as if they melted together, every smooth surface, every microscopic crease dissolving into one another.

When my mind came to, I pushed back. I shoved softly with the hand on his chest. I managed to pull my lips off of his, even though they seemed to stick together like fingers to fresh, dripping honeycomb.

"You okay?" he asked, a concerned look forming on his face.

I nodded and paused to think of what to say.

"I just… I don't want to risk anything this summer… with the trip and everything," I explained. "It's nothing you've done, I promise," I said, keeping my hand on his chest for just a moment longer, running it down the center line of his stomach before finally lifting it off.

"Oh…okay. Yeah, I get that," he said. He took a short step backward. "I'm sorry," he said. He shook his head at himself.

"No, it's okay," I assured him.

He took a couple steps backward and downed the rest of his drink. "I'm gonna go back to the bar. Wanna come?" he asked. I nodded. He started walking and then turned back, holding his free hand out for me. I took it and followed him back through the crowd.

Back at the bar, Wes gave my hand a squeeze and let go to sit down at one of the open chairs. I looked around and found Elena and Jack standing by a support beam a few feet from where Wes sat down.

"Hey! Did you see where Munro went?" I asked, walking up to them. I hoped it wasn't far. I needed to talk to him. Jack stood holding Elena around the waist as she continued to sway to the music and sip on her drink. Her curls bounced around her cheeks.

"He said he was going home," said Jack.

"Did he say why?" I asked, knowing exactly why. Jack shook his head.

Stars in the Honey

I looked around the club one more time and then took my spot next to Jack and Elena on the support beam.

I woke up in my room in the apartment to a knock on the door. I wasn't sure at first where the sound came from, so I searched the room for anything out of the ordinary: two tall windows on the back wall, a bedside table, a dark wood floor, a dresser, a desk with a TV, a shut, white closet door, and my suitcase. *Nothing.*

The knocking came again and right after, Wes peeked his head in the doorway. "Seren, you awake?" he whispered.

"I'm awake," I whispered back. I strained my eyes against the slivers of light breaking through the curtains into my dark room.

"Can I come in?" he whispered again.

"Mhm," I answered.

Wes opened the door all the way and shuffled in, closing it behind him. He walked over and sat on the edge of my bed, turning to face me. He wore the same clothes as he did last night.

I pulled my arms out from under the covers and rubbed my eyes. Little flecks of leftover mascara landed on my hands. "I'm glad you're home. I was worried last night when you weren't here when we got back," I said.

"Yeah. I'm sorry," he started. "I know I made it kind of awkward. Didn't I?" He still had the bandana from last night in his hair and his eyes seemed to only open halfway.

"No, I know it seemed like it, but I promise you, it's okay," I assured. It *was* okay. There was nothing between Munro and I…at least, nothing yet. It was just one date and it turned out horribly wrong. "I did owe you a raincheck after all," I reminded him, remembering prom night all over again.

He laughed softly. "That makes me feel a little better…but I know I'm not the one you want. I don't even know if you're the one I want…" he began, then he rolled his eyes at himself. "Actually, I don't know if that's true. I want you and I know it, but sometimes I feel that way and then my feelings change on a whim and I don't know what I want anymore and -"

"Wes, it's okay," I said, cutting him off before he ran out of breath on his rant.

He nodded. His fingers ran over the stitching in the comforter over my legs.

"I think you should talk to him," he said quietly. He avoided eye contact for what seemed like the first time ever.

I nodded, pulling the comforter closer to my face.

"I did have a good night though," he said.

I studied him. A half-smile formed on his solemn face.

"Me too," I agreed. "That kiss…" I started.

"It was awesome," he said, laughing wholly like his usual self, and it made me laugh too.

We sat through a silent moment, both just enjoying the other's company for a few seconds.

"Maybe one day," he stated. His eyes met mine and we shared a soft smile as I nodded. He looked around my room and then back at me. "Well, I'm hungry as hell. Wanna make breakfast with me?" he asked.

I nodded, flipped the covers off, and swung my legs over the side of my bed.

As we walked out of my room and into the living room, something crashed to the floor.

"Are you fucking kidding me?" Munro stood in the doorway between the kitchen and the living room with a plastic cup of water. He had dropped it when he saw us and a puddle formed at his feet.

"Goddamnit. Really, Wes?" he exclaimed.

"What?" Wes asked.

"I can't believe you! You knew I really liked her! What the hell!?" Munro screamed. I had never heard him raise his voice. It boomed straight from his chest through our eardrums.

"I didn't do anything," Wes tried explaining.

Munro grabbed his glass from the ground and turned back into the kitchen. "You are the absolute worst fucking friend, man. I thought I could trust you," he said from the kitchen.

Wes walked slowly toward the doorway.

"I'm telling you - "Wes began.

"No, Wes. I'm tired of being your quiet little side-kick. I'm telling YOU," he said pointing, "that you're an asshole."

I attempted to reason with him. "Munro, he's trying to tell you that nothing happened."

He stepped out of the kitchen and shoved past Wes. "If nothing happened, then why is he still in his club clothes? Why do you still have makeup on? You never sleep with makeup on," he said. His body didn't know what to do or where to go, so he kind of just turned back and forth in one spot, standing between Wes and I. "You know what? Both of you are awful people. You steal every girl I ever like. And you, I tried helping you the other day but you just pushed me away and then...then, you go and hook up with HIM." Munro stormed off past me, brushing his shoulder against mine. I felt his anger rush through me like lightning.

I sat down on the arm of one of the couches. My stomach clenched tight under my lungs. My fingers shook, tracing the faint pattern in the couch. "I have to leave," I told Wes. He watched silently as I stood up and made my way back to my bedroom.

As I got halfway through packing, Wes showed up in my doorway again. "Seren, please don't leave. I'm gonna explain everything to him. I'll make him listen," he said.

I didn't reply. Instead, I packed faster. I didn't bother folding anything, shoving piles of everything into the bag and the suitcase. I zipped them up.

Wes blocked the door with his body. I remembered how it felt pressed up against him last night. I remembered how good it felt in that moment and then a rush of nausea hit.

"Please, let me go," I said, feeling wobbly in my own feet.

"I really don't want to," he whispered.

"Let me go," I said, a little louder this time. I shook my head and moved forward, pushing my body into his. "Let me go, Wes," I repeated. He let his body move away from the doorway.

I walked a few steps into the living room and turned back to say, "Thank you."

He nodded solemnly.

I made it to just a couple feet in front of the apartment door and Elena walked out of her room.

"Where are you going?" she asked. She let out a long yawn.

I stopped but said nothing.

"Seren, are you leaving?" she asked. I could feel her presence getting closer to me.

"I have to," I said. I didn't face her.

"What's wrong? You don't have to leave, Seren," she said, starting to realize what was actually happening. "Don't leave. I can help with whatever's wrong…We can go talk, just you and me." I could hear the desperation forming in her voice.

It feels too much like home.

I turned and looked her in the eye. "I'm leaving." I felt the tears well up in my eyes and it stung as one tear dropped down my cheek. I turned and raced to the door, opening it, and shutting it as quickly as I could behind me.

"Seren! Please!" Elena yelled from inside. I heard her footsteps get closer to the door. "Seren!" she yelled again.

And then I ran.

Chapter 13

I walked down the Louisville streets after an hour of consoling myself in a gas station bathroom and persuading myself not to go back. The air was hot, making my shirt stick to every crease of my stomach, bending together in wet folds under my bra. After a couple hours, my feet had started to chaff in my flip-flops.

At the corner where two streets met, I stopped at a cafe for lunch. They exclusively sold sandwiches, all with meat, so I asked for a BLT without the B and added every other vegetable topping they offered. I sat in the stuffy cafe against the wall in a red booth that stuck to the back of my legs until they called my order number.

"244?" called an employee. Then he basically threw the plastic tray and sandwich up onto the counter.

Stars in the Honey

I got out of the booth, ripping the backs of my

thighs off in the process, and grabbed my sandwich.

"Thank you!" I called. Then I took my sandwich to go.

After another couple hours of walking, I could

have sworn my feet were bleeding so I stopped at a park

and found a bench to sit at. The park wasn't very big, just a

square of grass with a fountain and a few benches on each

side. I slipped off my sandals and inspected - no blood, but

I had some really nice blisters forming between my first

and second toes.

I sat on that bench for a few hours and during that

time, I witnessed a raccoon stealing leftovers from a trash

bag outside a hotel, a mom leave her twin babies outside in

a stroller to go *inside* a store and shop for twenty minutes,

and four skater guys attempt some kind of flip trick and all

fall on their faces, one right after another.

After another hour, I rummaged through my bag

for my book, when I found a bag of potato chips I had kept

from the last hotel's snack bar. I had shoved the sandwich

wrappings in my bag too because there wasn't a trashcan

around when I had finished it hours ago. The wrapping

paper was red and white checkered print. I turned and

faced the empty side of the bench, bringing my feet up and

crossing them the best I could without falling off the edge.

I unfolded the wrapping paper and set it down on

the bench. Then, I opened up the bag of chips and dumped

them onto the paper. I ate one chip and waited.

A family walked by. A little boy and a little girl

waved to me and I waved back.

I stared back at my picnic. "I know I'm a couple

days late..." I whispered, "But Happy Birthday, Mom."

A couple hours later, it was getting dark. The area

around the park had been vacated besides some kind of

creatures hanging out in the bushes and a homeless man

that fell asleep on the ground next to the fountain. I packed

up my things and started walking again.

Fuck, my feet hurt.

I pulled out my phone and tried to bring up my maps but the service wasn't good enough where I stood. So I kept walking.

After about five minutes, I found a few blocks on one street filled with little shops, a bar, and some nicer restaurants, so I stopped in front of one and tried again. I clicked open my phone which almost blinded me since the sun was now completely hidden behind the taller city buildings, ignored the messages and missed calls from the band, and scrolled through my apps to find the one that I needed.

Suddenly, my phone flew out of my hand and onto the street. It shattered, tiny shards of glass shooting out around the asphalt. And then my arms were pulled backward. I lost my balance, my legs coming out from under me as I was dragged back and into a dark alley. The sun didn't seem to ever reach that far.

I noticed a graffiti smiley face on the dark brick as my body was thrown against the side of a dumpster and forced to stay upright by a man in dark clothes. He wore a black beanie, pulled down far enough so I could barely see his eyes and a zip-up jacket that covered his entire neck and chin. Tiny red beard hairs like Wes' stuck out the top. The man grinned at me and all I noticed was the smell of his breath - it was like an ice cream treat that had sat in the sun too long and turned rotten.

I looked past the man and saw another, an almost identical of him scouring through my bag. Shadows covered the alley and the second man seemed to not have a face at all. The first man with the red beard leaned in, taking his time to linger around my neck as he scanned my expression.

He had his whole body pressed against mine. I tried moving one leg but it just felt numb. The other was stuck tight between the man's leg and the dumpster. I could feel the dumpster's lid slicing into the back of my neck. I turned my face to the side, trying to breathe in anything but the man's sickening breath.

A hand slid up my shirt. Calloused fingers scraped at my skin. A finger traced the underwire of my bra.

I didn't see anyone walk by the entrance of the alley. And if anyone did, they didn't stop to help.

"Come on, man. She's got nothing but a couple fives and a debit card," said the second man. He sounded like he smoked three packs a day. He started to walk off, dropping my bag and the useless items on the ground.

The man crushing me drew in a long breath. He leaned in again. This time his teeth grazed my ear and he said, "Sorry 'bout that, pretty lady."

He dropped me. My legs couldn't take the weight of my own body so I fell to the floor. I watched the man's boots walk out of the shadows and around the corner.

I held myself up with my hands but stared at the ground. The asphalt was covered in remnants of rainwater, glossy car oil, and bits of dirt and I'm sure, rat droppings too. I picked up one hand and wiped it off on my shirt. Then I reached around to the back of my neck. Dark orange blood stained my fingertips. I wiped them off on my shirt again.

I sat back now, against the side of the dumpster where the man had trapped my body before. I scanned the rest of me. First, I closed my eyes.

Breathe in. Breathe out.

I focused on what I could smell now.

Summer rain. Sweat. Garbage.

A hint of our bathroom after my mother miscarried.

I shook my head and opened my eyes. *Breathe in. Breathe out.*

I looked at my feet first. One flip-flop's strap was broken, hanging off on one side. I had the blisters between my toes and a couple scrapes, one on my heel and one that took off most of my pinky toe's skin. No blood.

Then I scanned up and down my legs. Both of my knees were scraped from the fall to the ground. A little blood.

My stomach and chest were fine, other than a lingering feeling of a man's touch.

My arms had a few red, risen scratches from the man's fingertips and the shove into the dumpster, but overall, fine.

My face was fine.

I felt a sting in my neck in some places and in others, it felt numb.

I wasn't sure if my legs would hold me yet, so I scooted myself across the asphalt to grab my bag and it's spilled contents from the ground. I dragged it all back to the dumpster and settled back down. So much of me wanted to leave that alley. But another part of me knew that the men weren't with me there anymore. They were somewhere out past the shadows and the shadows now felt somewhat comforting.

Stars in the Honey

My silver headscarf was left, tied around the handle of my bag. I untied it and wrapped it around my neck. It was a little tight. I could feel the pressure each time I swallowed, but it kept droplets of blood from trickling down to my back.

I zipped up my bag and tried to stand again. I was fine. My feet were sore, mostly from walking, but they held me up. And the scrapes on my knees bent and stretched as I left the alley, but I could still walk. I threw my bag over my shoulder and stopped before the streetlight met the alley shadows.

Breathe in.

Breathe out.

Chapter 14

I found my suitcase lying on its side in the gutter. I grabbed it, wiping off some of the muck it had accumulated, and stood it straight up. One wheel was broken but I dragged it down the street and into the first place I found that was still open.

I walked up three concrete steps and into a pub. It was pretty light inside, yellow-tinted fixtures above every little table and booth lining two of its walls. The shelves behind the bar lit up the colorful bottles of assorted liquor.

I trudged over to a booth and sat my suitcase and bag on one of the seats. A few older men, a biker gang and their wives, and the two bartenders all watched as I made my way slowly over to the bar. I must have looked ridiculous, scraped up all over, a weird scarf around my neck. I'm sure the blood could be seen through the fabric.

I squeezed my way between two bar stools and one of the bartenders leaned over to me. He had long blonde hair that reached his shoulders and had a fluffy beard. He seemed to be the youngest person in the bar, other than myself.

"Hi," I squeaked. "Do you have a phone I could borrow?"

The bartender nodded. "Of course. Take mine," he said. He pulled a leather jacket out from under the bar and a cell phone out of its pocket. "Passcode is 4153," he instructed and handed it over.

"Thank you," I said. I took the phone back to the booth, entered his passcode, and dialed a number.

It rang and rang and no one answered.

I tried again. It rang four times.

"Hello?" Elena's voice came over the line.

I couldn't say anything. Tears just started sputtering down my cheeks. Everyone in the bar was watching, but tried to seem like they weren't.

"Hello? Someone there?" she asked again.

"Yeah," I answered.

"Seren? Seren, is that you? Are you okay?" Her confusion turned to panic. "What's wrong? Where are you?" she asked.

I sobbed. An overwhelming breath of fresh air flowed through me at the sound of Elena's voice and I sobbed right into the phone in a dingy pub with everyone watching but pretending to not be watching me.

"Seren, please. Tell me where you are," Elena begged. I could hear the guys' voices in the background.

"Um, I'm not sure. Hold on," I said. I looked around the room. There was nothing indicating what pub I was in or what part of town I had walked to.

A few of the biker wives noticed me searching. One of them, wearing a Harley Davidson t-shirt and bright red lipstick, made eye contact with me.

"Hi, um, what is this place called?" I asked. My voice still strained to come out but she heard me.

"You're in Frank's Pub and Brewery, sweetie…on Todd St," she said. Her voice was gentle.

"Thank you," I said back.

"Elena?" I asked.

"I'm here," she replied.

"I'm at Frank's Pub and Brewery on Todd St."

"We'll be there as soon as we can," she said. "I promise."

We hung up.

After giving the bartender his phone back, I sat back in the booth and waited. The biker gang wife brought me a glass of water, and I drank a little. Then, her husband bought an order of mozzarella sticks and set it on my table too. He was a big man with a long graying beard and a big metal belt buckle with some kind of rabid animal embellished on it.

"Oh, I'm not really hung-" I started.

"We know where you're at right now," he said, his voice low and grumbly. His wife came up behind him and reached up to put her cheek on his shoulder. "You'll get where you need to be." He patted the table lightly and walked back to his group.

Forty-five minutes and four cheese sticks later, the band's van pulled up outside the pub. I started to get up and winced and the bartender noticed. He ran over quickly, dodging the tables and chairs in the middle of the room.

"Let me help," he said. He took one of my hands and held tight as I maneuvered out of the booth without touching any of my scrapes. When I stood, I noticed purple bruises forming on my knees.

"Thank you," I said. He nodded in return.

I looked back at the biker gang again. The wife was sitting on her husband's knee. Both sipped on beers.

"Can you do one more thing for me?" I asked the bartender.

"Of course," he replied.

I grabbed my bag and opened it, pulling out *Norwegian Wood.*

"Give this to them," I said, gesturing to the biker couple, "and tell them, 'thank you,' after I leave."

The bartender nodded and took the book. He studied the cover for a moment, nodded again, and made his way back to the bar.

I didn't have any money left. I didn't know if they liked to read. But I knew Elena liked it, and if she liked it, so would anyone.

I walked out of the bar and Elena stood patiently on the sidewalk next to the opened passenger side door of the van. She looked at me and started to smile, but after just a couple steps, it turned into a frown and in just seconds, she was crying.

"What happened to you?" she croaked out.

I walked to her, slowly, trying to conceal the limp. "I'm okay," I began as she wrapped her arms around my stomach. Over her shoulder, I could see Jack in the driver's seat and Munro and Wes in back through the windows.

"Some guys mugged me," I said, trying to keep it simple so she wouldn't ask too many questions.

"They mugged you? Are you sure you're okay? Did they hurt you?" she asked, pulling away and holding my arms in so she could look at my body standing still. "You have bruises and scratches everywhere."

"They're just scratches."

After she searched my body one more time, she helped me into the van. The ride to the apartment was silent. I didn't want to talk anyway.

At the apartment, I lied down in bed, partially because I was exhausted but also because Elena made me. She brought me hot tea. Chamomile, lemon, and honey. It felt like a hug from my father.

"Sleep. I'll be on the couch if you need me," she whispered, making sure the comforter was pulled all the way up to my neck.

"You don't have to-"I started.

"I am," she insisted. She patted down the comforter one more time and left the room, leaving my door slightly cracked.

Chapter 15

Elena came back in the next morning before I even woke up. I only knew that because she switched out the tea I had left from the night before for a new steaming cup and an extra little packet of honey. I sat up, poured the honey in, and took a deep breath of lemon scented steam. After a couple sips, she knocked and walked back in.

"Hey, how are you feeling?" she asked. She had changed out of her gig outfit from the night before into pajama shorts and a giant t-shirt.

"Fine. Sore...but fine," I said. I took another sip. Droplets of steam ran down the back of my nostrils, and I remembered all the nights in my bedroom at home where we'd sip tea and do yoga before bed.

"We have a gig later today. You should stay here though. And then we have all day tomorrow off, one more night here, and then we're leaving for Cincinnati," she said.

I nodded.

"Someone else wanted to say hi. That okay?" she asked.

I nodded again.

"Okay, yell or call me or text me if you need *anything*," she said. Then she walked out, leaving the door open this time.

I waited a moment, sipping more of my tea, and then Munro stepped in.

"Hey," he said, "can I come in?"

"Yeah," I answered.

He walked over to the bed and sat on the edge.

"You okay?" he asked. He twirled the rings around on his finger. His hair was tangled and his glasses only slightly covered up the dark purple circles under his eyes.

"Yeah… Are you?" I asked.

He smiled but said nothing.

"It's storming this morning. Did you notice?" he asked.

I shook my head.

"I remember you saying once that you liked storms," he said.

I nodded and slowly pulled the comforter off my body. Elena had forced me to change since my clothes were covered in everything in that alley. I had on long pajama pants and a loose tank top.

I walked over to the window. I could feel Munro staring at the back of my neck, where Elena had bandaged me up.

I looked out. Dark clouds moved swiftly across the sky and light rain sprinkled against the glass. We were so high up that the people walking in the streets were just blurry figures - no identities. They didn't seem real or even alive. Bikes flew by and in between cars, dodging death at every curve. I glanced back over my shoulder.

Munro fiddled with the edge of the comforter.

"Every time I try to leave and do something good for myself, I just get smacked in the face," I said, turning back to the window.

"Why do you keep leaving then?" he asked, his voice rolling out low like slowing train wheels.

"Because…I feel like I need something else," I said.

"Right. You said you needed to find yourself, but—" he started.

I turned around sharply. "Finding yourself is bullshit," I said. My neck stung. He looked up at me finally, eyes wide. "It's bullshit, Munro, and you know it. I'm already myself. I am every bit myself as I always have been and nothing is going to change that…not getting into college, not finding a good-paying job, not…" I paused watching his foot start to step forward toward me. "Not being with a nice boy."

"A nice boy? Is that all you think I am?" Munro sits back on the bed.

"I…no. It's not." I turned and leaned back against the window sill. I stared at the floor. My shadow lurked under me, like everything bad inside of me was staring right back. "I just…I thought that staying would get me stuck in something again. Like I was stuck in that stupid tiny town. Stuck where my mom left me."

"She didn't leave you there on purpose."

"How do you know that? What if I'm meant to stay in that same town with my practically mute dad in that library dusting off books for the rest of my life?"

Munro looked at me, scanning my face like he had done before hundreds of times. Then he patted the bed next to him. I walked over and sat down, making sure to stay a couple inches away. If I touched him, my skin would reject me and cause my whole self to give in and crawl into his arms in a crying mess.

He drew in a long breath. "I know that's not where you're supposed to be."

I said nothing and nodded toward the floor.

"And I know you might not necessarily want to hear this…but what if you're supposed to be with me?" he asked, pausing for just a moment. "Or maybe Wes, I don't know…" he trailed off. "Maybe Elena," he finished, a gentle smirk forming on his lips.

I looked up from the floor now and straight at him. He pursed his lips a bit, waiting for my reaction. I didn't give him one.

"What if people aren't necessarily supposed to be in a certain place or doing a certain thing…what if people are supposed to be with certain *people*. Me, Elena, the band…You're happy with us right?" he continued.

I thought for a moment and nodded again.

"Exactly. What if right now…at least in this part of your life, that's all that matters?" He reached over to me and placed one hand on my knee. I could feel the warmth seep through to my leg. "You're right about finding yourself. You don't need some fancy film school or job to define you. You are you already. And you can do whatever you want… Who cares if NYFA rejects you again? Me, Elena, Jack, and Wes…and your dad. We will all still be here. We'll all help you figure it out."

"So I should do it?" I asked.

"Yes, if that's what you want, if that's what makes you excited for something again. The worst that could happen is another red rejection letter."

I sat back on the bed. Munro watched me, his eyes following the curves of my legs, my hips, my stomach. I pulled my legs up and laid them across his thighs. Then I leaned into him, letting my cheek rest on his shoulder.

"How are you and Wes?" I whispered. I felt his neck move, tendons stretching.

"We're fine. Just a misunderstanding," he paused, "I'm sorry."

"Don't be," I said.

I pressed my cheek into him a little harder. He wrapped his arm around to my back and rubbed until I felt myself falling back asleep.

Chapter 16

I woke up alone in my bed again, under the covers. A note on my bedside table said, "Headed off to the gig. Didn't want to wake you. See you tonight."

The sun was almost set and it cast a dark orange glow through the window.

I grabbed my laptop out of the hidden pocket inside my suitcase and opened it up. I set it on my bed and typed "NYFA Admissions" into the search bar. A website popped up. I clicked on it. I stared at it for a moment - the red screen with NYFA printed in big letters at the top and a blue link that read, "Apply today."

I shook my head, shut my laptop, and climbed back under the covers.

The next morning, there was a knock on my door and then Wes strode in, carrying a big ceramic plate.

"Good morning. I thought you might like your favorite meal," he said. The room was dark but the window let in enough light that it was easy to see the plate held a big stack of peanut butter covered pancakes.

"Oh, thank you," I said. I sat up in bed.

"You are very welcome," he said, handing over the plate and a fork.

"Want some milk?" he asked.

I shook my head. "No, it's okay," I said, "How did the gig go last night?"

"It went really well," he said. Then a look of excitement crossed his face. "I forgot. Really late last night, Under the Radar posted a review of us online. It was great! They said we had 'unique sound waves'," he used air quotes, "whatever that means. And the writer even mentioned your scarf around my arm. He thought it was a tasteful touch."

"That's so great!" I said. I set the plate down on my bedside table and reached for a hug. He leaned over and wrapped his thick arms around me.

"Also, guess what?" he said.

I gave him a look instead of replying.

"I finished my song," he said.

"Really?" I asked.

"Yeah. I almost had it done but I couldn't think of words for the bridge and then the other night, I was so worried about you that I didn't know what to do and I just started writing." He paused and smiled at me shyly, for once. "I know it's cheesy, but you inspired me."

"Well...I better hear it soon then," I said. I picked my plate back up.

He stood up and started walking backward out of the room, "Don't worry, you will... whether you're still here with us... or wherever you decide to be." He nodded to me and left the room.

A few hours later, the band left to get lunch with Patrick and Frank. I still wasn't up for leaving the apartment, so I brought my laptop and a couple books out into the living room. I turned on the first music station I could find.

Duffy started to sing.

I watched the blurb roll across the screen that said, "'Enough Love' - Duffy (2008)."

Breathe in. Breathe out.

I set my laptop on my legs, opened it, and searched, "NYFA film."

After a couple hours of research and planning, I had started writing another essay. Two paragraphs in, I heard the click of the hotel door opening.

"Hey, you're up!" called Elena. She walked in carrying leftover boxes in one hand, and holding Jack's hand with the other. Jack smiled and took the boxes from her, veering off toward the fridge.

"How you feelin'?" asked Wes, trailing in behind them.

"Better," I said, nodding.

Elena ran over and squeezed me. I took in a breath of her optimism and comforting smell of home - the good part of home.

Then Munro entered, carrying another leftover box and a tiny paper bag. He searched the room and let his eyes linger on me for a bit. After a couple seconds he smiled and his eyes creased behind his glasses. "We got something for you," he said. He set the leftover box in the kitchen and walked over, handing the bag out to me.

"A present?" I asked, taking the bag into my hands. It was the size of a small letter and so light that I wondered if there was even anything hidden inside.

"We stopped at this little store near the restaurant," Elena said. She plopped down onto the couch and cuddled her body up to mine. "Open it."

I opened up the top of the bag and pulled out a single piece of white tissue paper. Inside was a necklace, a delicate gold chain with a tiny star pendant.

I didn't say anything for a while. At first, I think they thought I might have not liked it. But really, I loved it so much that I couldn't think of anything good enough to say. A simple 'thank you' would never be enough for everything they had done for me, let alone this beautiful gift.

"Munro saw it and remembered your nickname," said Elena. She wrapped her arms around my stomach and squeezed.

I looked up at Munro and he nodded. "It's you," he said.

"Our Little Star," Elena added. She giggled, knowing how silly it sounded coming from her mouth since it was really only our moms that ever called me it.

I could feel the tears rising to my eyes. "Thank you," I said. I shifted my body around, trying to distract myself from the overwhelming feeling.

"What do you think about watching a good movie? We've got the whole evening free," suggested Jack. "Any ideas?" he asked, directing the question to me.

"I've got one. Go get cuddled up in my room and I'll be there in a couple minutes," I said.

None of them had disagreed with anything I'd said the past few days, which was honestly starting to get on my nerves, but at this moment, it was perfect. They all shuffled into my room, leaving the door open for whenever I decided to join.

I came into the room carrying my laptop. I glanced at the start of my essay one more time, shut it, and set my laptop on the desk.

"What was that?" Elena asked from behind me.

"I'm sending in another application…"

Elena's mouth dropped as I turned around to her.

"…for the film program in New York. Maybe one in California too, actually. I've been looking into it and it seems like an interesting setup," I continued. "But don't worry, no more running. If it doesn't work out, I'll find something else, maybe something even better."

When I turned around from the desk, I took in the view. Elena laid in the bed, covers half drawn back for me to join, while all three boys cuddled up on the floor, leaning up against the mattress.

"Are you gonna tell your dad?" asked Jack.

"I'll call him tomorrow and explain everything. I think he deserves to know the whole truth finally," I answered.

I walked over to the bed and climbed in next to Elena, making sure not to kick anyone in the face in the process. Once I was settled under the blankets, Elena pressed play on the TV remote. *Dead Poets Society* started playing. When the title dissolved from the screen, I drew in a long breath, knowing that I would cry any moment and then, Elena wrapped her arm around my stomach and I knew that crying would be okay.

After the movie, everyone drifted off toward their own beds. I heard Elena and Jack make a pitstop in the kitchen, giggling to each other quietly as they opened cabinets looking for a late-night snack. Wes patted me on the head and winked, leaving Munro sitting on the floor waiting for his chance to say goodnight.

He turned, sitting up on his knees. I scooted my body as close to the edge as I could, head still on my pillow. He said nothing. His eyes scanned my face and he reached up to move a piece of my hair off my forehead and behind my ear.

I touched a finger to his cheek and traced his face, his eyebrows, his nose, his top lip. He closed his eyes. I moved my face closer, and on instinct, his lips parted slightly. My lips brushed against his. We sighed into each other, finally giving in to what we both had been waiting for. He reached his hands in to touch me, but instead let them lay on the bed in front of me. He was scared to hurt

me. After the kiss, he drew in a breath, and without

opening his eyes, he said, "Goodnight, Seren."

But before he could stand, I grabbed his wrist

gently and pulled. "Stay, please."

He nodded, finally opening his eyes. In the dark,

his features were even softer than normal but his eyes were

bright, reflecting all of the light they could find. He

climbed in bed behind me. His arms found their place

around my waist and his nose nuzzled deep into the side of

my neck, avoiding the bandage.

"Goodnight," I whispered back.

I waited for his breathing to slow and his fingers to

go limp. A soft snore escaped through his parted lips.

And then, I was alone, with just a golden honey

glow beaming through the half-open window shades and a

happy memory of peanut butter on pancakes.

The End

Kelsey Cantrell was born and raised in a small town in Indiana. She has a BA in English writing and film studies from DePauw University. She currently lives in Indianapolis. Stars in the Honey is her first novel.

IG - @kelsbby29

Website: kcantrellbooks.com